FAKE IT UNTIL IT'S REAL

TINA GALLAGHER & CISSY MECCA

Fake It Until It's Real: Brewhouse Book Club Series Book 1

By: Tina Gallagher

Published by Galsalla Press

Cover Design: Qamber Designs & Emporium

Editor: KRJ Editorial

For the friends who became family...
this one's for you.

the legend of the maplemoor moose

Before Maplemoor had brick storefronts and brewery lights, it began with a handful of families convinced they could build something worth keeping.

The first winter nearly finished them. The river froze early. Supplies ran thin. More than one family whispered about leaving before the snow buried their resolve entirely.

Then one morning, Graeme Lochwell saw it.

A moose at the edge of the clearing. Not charging. Not grazing. Just watching.

By dusk, half the settlement had seen it. By morning it was gone, but its tracks remained, pressed deep into the snow. They didn't lead away from Maplemoor. They circled it, as if the animal had walked the perimeter and decided the place was worth guarding.

No one left that winter.

The brewery rose the following spring. Homes followed. Then shops. Then generations.

Over the years, people have claimed to see the moose again, near the riverbank, reflected in a window when life feels uncertain.

They call him the Maplemoor Moose.

Some say he appears when someone is thinking about leaving. Others say he shows up when a person needs reminding that where they're standing might already be home.

In Maplemoor, the moose isn't a story. He's a reminder.

Stay. You belong here.

"I'M JUST SAYING," Carli said, leaning forward, "if you spend enough time pretending to be into someone, it's not that shocking when feelings show up."

I took a sip of my coffee, letting the heat linger against my mouth longer than usual.

"That's still not how emotions work," Leeta replied flatly. "That's how convenience works."

A small smile tugged at my mouth as I set my mug down, but I stayed quiet and listened to them argue about the lives of fictional characters.

Around us, The Brewhouse buzzed the way it always did on the last Wednesday of the month for book club—alive without being loud. I liked nights like this. The kind where I could sit and blend into the rhythm of the room, listening more than talking, letting the world move around me without asking anything in return.

"I loved how Evie didn't just melt when she met Tris. She held her ground and made him work for it," Mallory said. "And I also liked that this one wasn't just about attraction. She and Tris had real stakes with their restaurants and families."

"I actually liked Tristano a lot," Carli said. "He doesn't just talk a good game. He steps up for Evie."

Tiff nodded. "Right? But Evie isn't some passive heroine."

"It helps that their fake romance doesn't stay fake for long," Ilona added, grinning.

We'd pushed four high-top tables together a couple of hours ago, claiming our usual space in the corner. Now the tabletops were cluttered with empty mugs, crumb-filled plates, and dog-eared paperbacks.

My gaze drifted, landing—like it always did—on the Maplemoor Moose figurine by the register, sporting its tartan scarf.

"What about you, Jess?" Maggie asked, pulling my attention back to the table. "You've been quiet tonight. What'd you think of the book?"

There wasn't a format to book club, but Maggie did like hearing at least one thought from each of us. I hadn't given mine yet. I looked down at my book.

"I liked it," I said. "The writing was great. The characters felt real. But fake dating has never been my favorite trope."

"Why?" she asked.

I shrugged. "I just find it hard to believe. Like, these people don't have feelings for each other, then they pretend to date, and suddenly they're in love." I gestured toward Leeta. "Like she said, that's not how emotions work. Unless there was something already there, I'm not sure how pretending to date makes it real."

Tiff snorted. "I don't know, Jess. A lot of times the chemistry's already there before people realize it. Spending time together just brings out what was already underneath."

Alexis nodded, ever the mediator. "I kind of agree with both of you. I don't always buy fake dating either, but I think proximity changes how people see each other. When you're around someone long enough, you stop skimming the surface, and suddenly you're paying attention."

"I think it worked because they kept choosing each other," Emily said. "Even after it started as a lie."

Leeta raised an eyebrow. "Still feels like a stretch."

Carli grinned. "That's romance, though. We're here for the stretch."

Maggie, who had been listening quietly from the end of the table, finally spoke. "I think it worked because the story made me believe *why* they fell. Not just that they did."

That earned a few murmurs of agreement.

This—right here—was my favorite part. The back-and-forth. The way no one had to agree, but everyone still felt heard.

Most of these women had known each other for years. Some longer than that. They had shared history and inside jokes and the kind of shorthand that came from showing up for each other over time. It would have been easy to feel like the add-on, the newest chair pulled up to an already full table—especially after leaving my own people behind.

But from the first night I'd shown up, no one had treated me that way.

I'd been coming to book club every Wednesday since I was invited, not long after I moved into The Lochwell. We only discussed a book the last week of the month. Every other week was more of a coffee klatch. Not everyone tore through books the way I did.

The last of the discussion wrapped up with a few final

thoughts on *My Foolish Heart*. Maggie pulled up the list on her phone to decide next month's pick.

When that was done, the energy shifted. Conversations splintered into smaller groups, voices overlapping.

Leeta leaned closer. "Are we still on for Saturday?"

"As long as the weather doesn't change," I said. "I hate hiking in the rain."

"Same." She chuckled. "But I think we're good."

"Breakfast here first?"

"Sounds good."

Maggie clinked her fork gently against her mug, and the table quieted.

"Before we go," she said, smiling at me, "I want to raise a toast."

The attention shifted, and my stomach gave a small, unexpected flip.

"Tonight marks three months since Jess moved to Maplemoor."

Three months. I blinked, surprised by the number. I'd stopped counting. At some point, I didn't need to count the days anymore. Life here had its own rhythm, and I'd slipped into it without noticing.

There were smiles, a few soft cheers, and a wolf whistle from Tiff.

"She came to Maplemoor for a new start and to figure out what comes next. And instead of hiding, she jumped right into the community and became one of us."

My throat tightened just enough to surprise me.

When I'd left my old life behind, I'd hoped for this part. The community. The way people showed up for each other.

"To Jess," Maggie said.

"To Jess," the table echoed.

I lifted my mug, warmth spreading through me.

"Thanks," I said. "I'm really glad I'm here."

My phone buzzed just as I set my mug down.

Nicole's name lit up the screen, and when I swiped to answer, her face appeared.

"Hey," I said. "The book club was just toasting my three-month-aversary. Say hi."

I turned the phone so she could see the ladies.

"Hi, everyone," Nicole said through the speaker.

A messy chorus of hellos followed, voices bumping into each other across the table.

I turned the phone back toward me. Nicole had shifted closer to the camera, her expression tight in a way that made my stomach drop.

"Is everything okay?"

"Jess," Nicole said, her voice quieter now. "Can you go somewhere private for a minute?"

"Sure." I pushed back from the table and stood. "I'll be right back," I said to the table as a whole, and headed outside.

I dropped into the nearest chair. "What's up?"

"I wanted you to hear this from me," Nicole said, her voice gentler than usual.

"You're freaking me out a little, Nic."

Nicole exhaled softly. "I know. I'm sorry."

"Just tell me."

"Brett's engaged," she said. "She'll be with him at the wedding."

The words didn't land right away. They hovered, waiting for me to catch up.

Something dropped in my chest. Not pain, exactly. More like the floor shifting an inch when you didn't expect it.

"Are you okay?" Nicole asked. "Jess?"

"Engaged?" I said. "Like...*engaged?*"

"Yes."

"We've only been broken up for nine months."

"I know."

Eleven years. My entire twenties and then some.

"We were together for eleven years."

Nicole nodded. "I know."

Her image blurred on the screen. Across the patio, moths circled the lamp post in lazy loops. I watched them until my eyes stopped burning.

Seeing Brett at the wedding was always going to be uncomfortable.

Now it would be torture.

CHAPTER TWO

caleb

BY THE TIME I got to The Brewhouse, my shoulders were reminding me it had been a long day of crawling around mechanical rooms and hauling gear.

All I really wanted was to get home, peel out of my work uniform, and let a hot shower do whatever it could for the knots between my shoulders.

But my sister Emily's text had delayed those plans.

Chicken chili's the soup of the day.

I'd told her to have Vee set a quart aside and that I'd swing by to grab it. It was definitely worth the detour.

I cut the engine and glanced over at Murphy.

"You ready?"

His tail thumped once against the seat.

"Yeah," I said. "Me too."

I stepped out of the truck and rolled my shoulders as I walked around to the passenger side. Murphy hopped down, and I clipped the leash onto his collar.

Vee had once commented that he had better manners than half the town.

Still, rules were rules. And at The Lochwell, dogs had to be leashed unless they were in the dog park.

Murphy and I walked around to the side of the building, and when we reached the patio, he lowered himself onto the concrete. I looped his leash around the railing.

"Back in a minute."

He yawned and rested his chin on his paws. He'd had a long day, too. Doggie daycare is exhausting.

I reached for the door, then glanced across the patio.

"Hey, Jess."

She looked up. "Hi."

Something in her tone caught my ear.

"You okay?"

"I'm fine," she said, her voice sharp.

I can take a hint.

"Have a good night."

She looked back down at her phone as I headed inside.

Vee was at the counter talking to a customer. She caught my eye, and I lifted a hand in a quick wave. She nodded back and continued talking.

I headed toward Emily.

"There he is," she said. "I thought you would have been here an hour ago."

"I got stuck in traffic."

I shifted my weight, the fabric of my uniform stiff against my shoulders.

Emily made a face. "You smell like work."

"Maybe because I was working."

"Well, you stink."

"Again, I worked."

"You always work."

"Do I always stink?"

"Yes." She wrinkled her nose. "All boys are smelly."

"Don't worry, I'm not staying," I said. "Murphy's outside."

"Of course he is," Emily said, "being better behaved than you."

I shifted my weight. "Thanks for the heads-up about the chili."

"I know it's your favorite."

"That's why you're my favorite sister."

"Low bar," she said. "Nora lives a state away. She's out of the loop on your favorite foods."

"Either way, you saved me from fast food. The last thing I want to do after a long day is cook."

"Where are you working again?" she asked.

"Just outside Waypoint. They're renovating the old jail into a restaurant, speakeasy, and boutique hotel."

"You're working on the old jail conversion?" Jess asked as returned and she slid into her seat.

"Yeah."

"My firm did the engineering for that," she said. "I actually wrote the proposal."

"Then you know what a nightmare it is."

"It's challenging."

I glanced at Emily. "That's engineer-speak for shitshow."

"Is it that bad?" she asked Jess. "Sometimes he's a baby."

"It's a tough one. He's not exaggerating."

"The building is so solid," I said. "Too solid. Every time we think we've got a clean run, it reminds us it was built to keep people inside and survive the apocalypse."

Jess laughed. "That tracks."

"It'll be good when it's done," I added. "It's just making us work for it."

My stomach chose that moment to growl, loud enough that Emily snorted.

"Wow," she said.

"I should probably feed myself before that gets any more dramatic."

"I'm going to head out, too," Jess said, standing. "I have an early camera-on Zoom tomorrow, so I need to look semi-human."

I said goodbye to Emily, then waved to the table. "Night, everyone."

A few goodbyes came back at me, casual and overlapping. I turned toward the counter, the pastry case already catching my eye. Long day or not, I wasn't leaving without something sweet to go with the chili.

Vee glanced up as I approached and reached beneath the counter before I even said anything. She set a quart container down between us.

"Good thing Emily told me to set this aside," she said. "The pot's almost gone."

"That would've been tragic," I said.

"Damn," Jess said from behind me. "I was hoping to grab some for lunch tomorrow."

"Hold on," Vee said. She walked toward the kitchen door and pushed it open. "Hey, do we have any chicken chili left back there?"

There was a pause, then a muffled response.

"Okay," she said, turning back. "I've got a pint."

Jess's shoulders relaxed. "I'll take it."

"It's yours," Vee said to Jess, then looked back at me. "Anything else?"

I glanced at the case. "I'll take a couple brownies, a chocolate chip cookie, and a Rice Krispies treat."

She put everything into a bag, dropped a small container on top, then pointed to it.

"There's some bacon in there for Murphy."

"You spoil him," I said as I tapped my card to pay.

"He deserves it."

Vee slid the bag toward me, then looked at Jess.

"Anything besides the chili?"

"No, that's it."

I said one final goodbye and headed out the door.

Murphy stood when he saw me, and I unlooped his leash from the rail.

"Come on, big guy. Let's head home."

We'd only taken a couple of steps when the door opened behind us. He paused at my side, ears raised, as Jess stepped onto the sidewalk. His tail gave a slow, hopeful sweep.

"Go on," I said, loosening my grip on the leash.

He didn't need a second invitation.

Jess crouched automatically, one hand reaching out. "Hi, handsome."

Murphy leaned into her like he'd been waiting all night for that exact moment, tail wagging harder now. She laughed softly and scratched behind his ears.

"He's such a sweetheart," she said. "What kind of dog is he again?"

"German shepherd, Irish setter mix."

"I always think he's some kind of Lab."

"Yeah, the shepherd is totally missing. To me, he just looks like a black setter."

Jess chuckled when Murphy lay down and rolled over so she could pet his belly. Of course she complied.

"All right, it's time to get going," I said to Murphy, then looked at Jess. "He'll have you here all night."

She gave him one last rub before standing.

"Sorry about earlier," she said. "That wasn't about you."

"No worries."

She smiled. "Good night, Caleb."

"Night."

She took a few steps away from us. Murphy sat up, but stayed where he was, looking between the two of us like he was weighing his options.

"Let's go, Murph. My chili is getting cold." I started toward my truck. Instead of following, Murphy hesitated, which isn't something he usually does. I shook my head and chuckled. "Seriously?"

Jess walked back to press a kiss to the top of his head. "Good night, Murphy."

He soaked it in, then stood and followed me toward the truck. I unclipped his leash and he jumped into the back seat.

I settled behind the wheel, then set my bag on the passenger seat and started the engine. Instead of settling in like he usually does, Murphy sat and stared at The Lochwell.

"Not happening, buddy."

He sighed and settled onto the seat.

CHAPTER THREE

THE BREWHOUSE FELT different on weekends.

Louder, mostly. More bodies, more laughter, the kind of energy that spilled out the door instead of settling into corners. Weeknights were for laptops and quiet conversations, for book club and familiar faces. Weekends belonged to everyone else—hikers in leggings, couples in baseball caps, and a few regulars who looked like they'd been awake since dawn on purpose.

I still didn't understand those people.

Leeta set her water bottle on the table like she was marking territory. "Okay," she said as we got into line. "Breakfast, coffee, and then we're out before I talk myself into going home and reading in bed."

"I support both plans," I said.

"You would. You're a professional reader."

"Can't argue with that," I said with a smile. "But I do make myself get out for a walk every day."

The truth was, there was a book waiting for me in my apartment. One I could have happily disappeared into. But I'd learned something in the last three months—Maplemoor had a way of making you feel like life was happening right in front of you.

I'd felt it the first time I visited during one of the town's festivals. People here waved you over instead of pushing past you, and conversations didn't end at polite small talk.

Between impromptu hikes, book club meetings that turned into late-night conversations, and people who noticed when you didn't show up, staying home felt less like rest and more like opting out. If I'd just wanted to disappear into my own life, I could've done that anywhere. Choosing Maplemoor meant choosing not to.

"What are you getting?" she asked, not taking her eyes off the menu.

"Avocado toast and a side of hash browns," I said. "You?"

"I'd love a cheese danish, but then I'd be starving within the hour. So I'm going with a bacon, egg, and cheese bagel."

The line moved fast, and within minutes we were sitting down with our food.

I took my first sip of coffee and groaned.

"Vee makes the best blends. I'm seriously addicted."

"So is half the town," Leeta said, then took a bite of her sandwich.

We didn't talk while we ate, but it was a comfortable silence. Leeta had a calm, practical kind of presence. She wasn't the loudest in the book club, wasn't the one driving the discussion or cracking the biggest jokes, but she was steady. The kind of person who listened with her whole face.

When we tossed our trash and stepped outside, the air was fresh. May had finally committed to spring. The sun was warm without being pushy about it, and the breeze smelled like damp earth and new leaves.

Leeta pulled her sunglasses down from the top of her head. "Perfect hiking weather."

"Unless it changes," I said automatically.

She made a face. "Don't put that into the universe."

We drove a short distance out of town, parked at a trailhead that looked like it belonged on a postcard and started up the path. It was the kind of hike that wasn't trying to kill you but also didn't let you forget you were using muscles.

For the first stretch, I followed behind her, enjoying the sounds of nature. Birds, wind, the occasional crunch of gravel under our shoes. Somewhere off to the side, water moved over rock, steady and patient.

I was glad I hadn't canceled on Leeta. Moving felt better than staying home with my thoughts.

I'd stared at my ceiling longer than I cared to admit, knowing the bachelorette trip was only days away and the wedding itself was just a couple of weeks out. Since Nicole's bombshell, the whole thing had shifted from a series of celebrations into a countdown I couldn't escape.

When the trail widened, Leeta slowed until I was at her side. We walked like that for a few quiet steps before she spoke.

"Okay," Leeta said after a few minutes. "How's it feeling?"

"Good," I said. "My cardio's definitely better since I started walking every day."

Leeta shot me a look, brow raised.

"I meant everything," she said. "New town. New routines. New people."

"It's good," I said. And it was. That was what kept surprising me. "Still a little weird, sometimes. Like I'm borrowing someone else's life and waiting for my real one to come back."

Leeta nodded once, like she understood exactly what I meant.

"I just didn't expect it to be this easy to fit in," I said. "Which probably sounds ridiculous."

"It doesn't," she said. "It's Maplemoor. We like collecting people."

The way she said *we* made my chest tighten a little.

I laughed, needing the release. "Is that the town slogan?"

"It should be."

The path widened, and the trees thinned enough that I slowed without meaning to. Sunlight poured through the leaves like it was generous with itself.

I stopped for a second, hands on my hips, breathing it in. The words slipped out before I could second-guess them.

"When Brett broke up with me, I was wrecked," I said. "One minute I was planning our future, and the next I was figuring out how to pack up a life I thought was mine."

"I'm glad you ended up here." She reached out and squeezed my hand. "We don't have to talk about it," she added, "but we can, if you want."

I started walking again and let that settle between us for a few steps, then I shook my head once, almost like I could physically clear the heaviness.

"It's a beautiful day," I said, gesturing at the sunlit trees, the trail, and the whole world that felt like it was finally waking up. "And I've spent enough time commiserating about Brett."

"That's fair," Leeta said. "But if you ever want to vent, I'm here."

"I appreciate that." I exhaled, relieved at the shift. "Let's talk about something shallow. Or fun. Or both."

"Tell me about your upcoming trip."

I smiled despite myself. "We're going to Savannah."

"Nice."

"It's a classy bachelorette," I said. "We left our get-drunk-and-pass-out era behind a few years ago."

"Have all of them?"

"Nicole and I have," I said. "I'm assuming the rest will behave."

Leeta laughed. "So what happens at a classy bachelorette?"

"Shopping," I said, ticking it off. "Spa treatments. A wine tasting or two. And dinners where we wear real clothes and nobody ends up crying in a bathroom."

"That's a low bar," Leeta said.

"And yet," I replied, "not always achievable."

We crested another small rise, and ahead the trail leveled out again. The sunlight made the leaves look almost neon, like the whole forest had been highlighted.

Leeta's tone shifted slightly, casual but pointed. "Are you excited?"

"Yeah," I said. "I'm looking forward to it."

"And the wedding?" she asked.

"It should be fun," I said. "I'll get to see a lot of people I haven't in a while. Nicole's family. Old friends." I kept my voice steady, like saying it that way might make it true. "I just wish Brett wasn't part of it."

Leeta glanced at me. "He's in it, right?"

"Yeah," I said with a sigh. "My goal is to show up, focus on my maid-of-honor duties, smile, and disappear before anyone can treat me like an awkward footnote."

Leeta's gaze stayed on the trail, but her voice softened. "I'm sure your friends don't see you that way."

I thought about the months after the breakup—how

every dinner invitation came with careful eyes, and every *How are you?* felt loaded.

"Maybe not," I said.

"Are you bringing a plus-one?"

"No," I said. "I want to be able to come and go without worrying about anyone else."

She bumped her shoulder into mine and draped an arm around me for a second, warm and solid, then let it drop like it was no big deal.

The trees thinned until the view stretched out in front of us—layers of green hills, the river cutting through them like a ribbon.

Even if I wanted to, I wouldn't know who I'd bring.

caleb

MURPHY HIT the ground running the second I opened the truck door.

He launched himself out like he was late for something important, paws skidding on gravel, nose already down and working overtime. His tail whipped back and forth as if the trail had personally invited him.

"Okay, okay," Luke said, laughing as he climbed out of his side of the truck. "We get it. You're excited."

We followed him up the path and watched as he paused every few feet, looking back at us, ears perked, making sure we were still coming.

"He looks like he's been waiting for this."

I hated how true that was.

"Yeah," I said. "Work's been a lot of long days. Too many of them."

Murphy darted into the brush like he'd discovered something life-changing.

Luke watched him for a second. "That your way of saying you've been neglecting your dog?"

"I wouldn't say neglecting."

Murphy trotted back, proudly carrying a stick twice his size. I made a show of admiring it, and his tail wagged harder, clearly pleased with himself. Then he turned and was off again, prize held high.

Luke smirked. "I think he would."

I started down the trail, Luke falling into step beside me. "That's why we're here."

We watched the dog explore the tree line while balancing the stick. The woods were bright in that late-morning way, sunlight filtering through new leaves that were still figuring themselves out.

"How long will he carry that stick?"

"It depends on what else catches his attention."

Just then, Murphy froze.

Not stiff. Not alert-alert. Just...paused.

He sniffed the air once, slow and deliberate, his tail giving a single sweep before picking up speed.

I followed his line of sight and spotted Leeta and Jess heading down the trail toward us. Jess's hands moved as she talked, her cheeks pink, ponytail swaying.

"Murph," I said.

He sat and looked over his shoulder at me like he always did, but he was practically vibrating.

Jess noticed him and smiled.

"Go on." That's all I had to say before he dropped the stick and took off.

Jess laughed as Murphy skidded to a stop in front of her, tail wagging so hard it looked like it might knock him over.

"Well hello to you," she said, crouching to pet him.

He leaned into her, looking like he was in heaven.

Luke let out a low whistle. "Wow."

I gave him a "don't start" look before continuing toward them.

"I think he's decided we're best friends," Jess said when we reached them, scratching under Murphy's chin.

"Seems that way."

Murphy flopped onto his side so she could pet his belly.

Jess's grin lit up her face, making her even more breathtaking. "Oh my God. He just escalated this."

"He has no shame," I said with a chuckle.

"He's a sweetheart."

"That's how he gets away with everything."

Luke and Leeta fell into easy conversation and I stayed where I was, watching Murphy soak up the attention like he'd been starved for it.

Leeta pointed between Luke and Jess. "Do you two know each other?"

"No, but it seems Murphy and Caleb do."

Jess lifted her hand in a small wave without stopping the belly rub. "Jess Harper."

"Luke Ward," he said. "Nice to meet you."

"Same."

Conversation drifted the way it always does in a small town. And of course, Murphy made himself the center of it.

After a few minutes, Leeta glanced at her watch. "We should get going."

Jess stood, brushing her hands on her leggings. "It was good to see you," she said, giving Murphy one last scratch.

"You too," I said, although she was probably talking to Murphy.

We all said our goodbyes and they continued down the trail. Murphy watched them for a second, then ran ahead to explore again.

Luke waited exactly three seconds.

"Well, that was interesting," he said.

"Don't."

"That dog just met the love of his life."

"He met a woman who scratches his belly."

"Same thing."

"She lives at The Lochwell, right?"

"Yeah. She's in Emily's book club."

"And Murphy obviously likes her."

"I'm not being set up by my sister or my dog."

Luke snorted, but it faded fast. He kicked a rock off the edge of the trail and watched it disappear into the brush.

"You know Mom worries about you."

"I know."

"She thinks you're going to end up alone."

"With this family?" I said. "Unlikely."

"That's what I told her."

Murphy burst through a patch of brush and came back with another stick, smaller this time, but still worthy of presentation.

Luke laughed. "When was the last time you went on a date?"

I opened my mouth, then closed it. If I told him the answer, I'd never hear the end of it. Instead, I said, "That's not relevant."

Luke winced. "Yeah, that means it's been too long."

"I just haven't met anyone I want to go out with recently."

He grunted in response, but I knew the discussion wasn't over. And of course, I was right. I only got to enjoy the sounds of nature for a few minutes before he said, "It just seems like you haven't put yourself out there since Rachel left. And that was what, five years ago?"

"Yeah," I said. "But I have tried. It's just crazy out there."

"Haley has a co-worker she's been dying to—"

I cut him off before he could finish.

"I'm done with setups in general."

"Why?"

"Because I always end up feeling like an asshole when it doesn't work out."

"Maybe this woman will work out."

"That's highly doubtful."

"What about dating apps?"

"I'm done with those too," I said. "I don't need that kind of crazy in my life."

"Bad experiences?"

I ticked them off on my fingers.

"One woman tried to move into my house after two weeks. Another was live-streaming our date and didn't tell me. I figured it out when she asked me to repeat something and looked at her phone instead of my face."

Luke snorted. "You're kidding."

I held up my right hand as if I was swearing.

"Oh, one told me I'd have to get rid of Murphy if I wanted a future with her."

Luke glanced at Murphy. "Seriously?"

I looked him dead in the eye. "After the second date."

His loud laugh echoed through the trees and had Murphy looking back at us long enough to make sure we were okay.

"And I'm sure you remember the one who scratched the hell out of me during sex. I looked like I'd been attacked by a feral cat."

Luke doubled over laughing. "Fuck, I forgot about that."

"So I'm done. It's not worth my time and energy."

Luke wiped his eyes. "Mom's worried about you ending up alone, but I'm worried your dick's going to atrophy."

"I would rather jerk off the rest of my life than need medical attention after sex."

Luke snorted. "You know the perfect woman isn't just going to fall into your lap, right?"

I shrugged. "Maybe not."

He waited, like he expected more.

"But if I meet someone, I meet someone," I added. "And if I don't, I'm not interested in forcing it."

Luke studied me for a second, then nodded once. "Fair enough."

Murphy bounded ahead, jumping over roots and nosing into the brush like every inch of the trail was personally designed for him. Sunlight flashed across his back as he moved, the kind of effortless happiness you couldn't fake.

Luke sobered a little. "You okay, though? Really?"

"Yeah," I said, and I meant it. Mostly. "I just...I don't want to do that again."

"Rachel?"

I didn't answer.

"I heard she might be back. Or might be moving back."

I kept walking.

He waited. "Is there a chance—"

"No," I said before he could finish. "It took me too long to get over her to open that door again."

Luke shrugged. "I'm just saying—it's been five years."

"She didn't want what I had to offer back then. I don't see why that would be different now."

"Fair," he said. "But if she's moving back to Maplemoor, I'm figuring the grass wasn't greener. So don't be surprised if she comes knocking on your door."

We reached a clearing, sunlight spilling through the trees, the trail opening wide. Murphy circled back toward us, panting, tongue lolling, a big smile on his face.

Whatever Rachel's doing back in town wasn't any of my concern.

Murphy trotted ahead, tail high, like he'd never once questioned whether his life was enough.

I had a good dog, a solid life, and a trail still ahead of me.

For now, that felt like plenty.

CHAPTER FIVE

THE HOUSE WAS QUIETER than it had been all weekend, the kind of quiet that settles in once the laughing burns itself out. Earlier, it had been full of candlelight, clinking glasses, and endless conversation. The personal chef we'd hired for the night had moved through the kitchen, plating courses of small plates that looked almost too pretty to eat.

Almost.

We'd managed anyway.

Nicole had wanted a classy bachelorette, and we'd delivered.

Now the kitchen was clean, the dishes loaded into the dishwasher, and the girls had drifted off one by one—Tara first, then Maya and Sasha, Lauren last after a dramatic yawn and a reminder that we were "not twenty anymore."

Nicole and I lingered.

"One more?"

"Absolutely."

She poured the rest of a Malbec into two glasses, nudging one toward me. I grabbed it and followed her outside to the back porch. We settled onto cushioned chairs overlooking a courtyard strung with soft white lights. The warm Savannah air carried the faint scent of jasmine and night-blooming flowers I couldn't name.

Nicole leaned back with a sigh. "Okay. I just need to say it."

I smiled. "You're getting married?"

She laughed, bumping her knee against mine. "Besides that."

"This weekend was perfect. Every minute of it," she said. "Thank you. You did an amazing job."

"I had help."

"You always deflect," she said. "I know you planned most of what happened here."

"I'm good at logistics." I shrugged. "And you're easy to celebrate."

Her expression softened. "Still. Thank you."

We clinked glasses and took a drink.

For a minute, we just sat there, listening to the cicadas and the distant hum of the city. Somewhere down the block, music thumped from a passing car, a reminder that Savannah didn't slow down just because we were sitting still.

The slideshow we'd watched earlier replayed in my mind. Nicole at five, missing her front teeth. Brian with braces and a bowl cut. Awkward college pictures, the night they met, the slow progression from friends to something more.

Love with a paper trail.

She tilted her head toward me. "How's Maplemoor?"

"I love it," I said without hesitation.

"Really?"

"I'll be honest...when I decided to move there, I thought

I was just running," I admitted. "From everything. I figured I'd live there a couple of years and figure out where I wanted to settle for real." I looked down and focused on my finger tracing the rim of the wine glass. "But it doesn't feel like that anymore. It feels like I landed somewhere, and I don't want to leave."

She smiled. "Tell me about it."

"The building I live in, The Lochwell...it's like a real community. People look out for each other, and it feels safe."

"Safe is underrated."

"Extremely," I said. "And the book club has become the hub of my social life."

"With how much you love reading, that doesn't surprise me at all."

"The thing is—we only talk about books one day a month," I said. "Every other time, it's basically a standing weekly check-in. We talk about everything and nothing and just...show up." I shrugged. "I know I'm not making it sound like anything special, but it really is. The book club, The Lochwell, and the whole town have welcomed me in a way I didn't expect."

Nicole's gaze softened. "That sounds like exactly what you needed."

"Yeah," I said quietly. "It kind of was."

She took a drink, then rolled her wineglass between her palms, eyes fixed on the liquid like it might rearrange itself if she waited long enough.

"But I'd be lying if I said I didn't miss you being within walking distance. Just texting and saying, *come over*, and you actually could."

"I know," I said. "That was the hardest part about leaving Philly. Knowing I was giving that up."

"Still," she said, "it sounds like you landed in the right place."

I nodded once, staring out at the courtyard lights. We sat there in the quiet, the kind that didn't rush to be filled.

After a moment, she looked at me again.

"So," she said gently. "How are you really doing?"

I knew what she was asking.

"I'm good," I said, giving her my automatic response to that question.

She leaned closer and looked me in the eye.

"How. Are. You. Doing?" she repeated.

I let out a slow breath. "I'm not going to lie," I said. "It stings."

We'd always said we'd get married once we were more established financially.

Nicole didn't say anything. She just waited for me to continue.

"We were together for eleven years," I said. "And we lived together for eight of those. That's not nothing." I exhaled, slow and deliberate. "When he ended it, Brett said marriage wasn't something he believed in anymore."

Nicole's jaw tightened, just slightly.

"And now, he meets someone and gets engaged within nine months."

As soon as the words were out of my mouth, a sense of dread hit. My stomach dipped, like I'd missed a step I should've seen.

My eyes widened. "Wait, was he—" I made a vague motion with my hand, unable to finish the thought. "With her? While we were still together?"

Nicole shook her head immediately. "No, I would've told you," she said. "They met at the gym a few months ago."

I nodded, relief flickering through me, followed by annoyance that I'd let my mind go there at all.

"What's her name?" I asked.

"Tabitha Banks," Nicole said. "But she goes by Tabby."

"What's she like?"

"She's... nice," Nicole said carefully. "Younger."

"How young?"

"Twenty-four."

Twenty-four.

Met at the gym.

Goes by Tabby.

My brain created an image of the woman before I could stop it—petite, cute, effortless. The kind of woman who looked like she belonged everywhere without trying. I hated that my mind went there, especially when I knew better than to play the comparison game.

I took a sip of wine, mostly to stop my thoughts from spilling out.

In my mind, I knew I was better off. Unfortunately, knowing didn't make my thoughts any quieter.

Brett getting engaged was never going to be fun news. But stacked on top of Nicole's wedding, it made everything that much heavier.

If the bachelorette weekend was any indication, the wedding would require more energy than I had. Everything this weekend had been smoothed over a little too carefully, like no one wanted to risk pressing on a bruise.

Like there was an unspoken agreement to keep everything bubbly—because if the mood dipped, I might go with it. The thought of carrying that through an entire wedding weekend was more than I wanted to think about.

"I know this isn't easy," Nicole said.

"It'll be fine." I smiled. "I can handle seeing him. I just don't want to be monitored by the entire guest list."

Nicole grinned. "I promise to be so stunning that all eyes will be on me the entire time."

I laughed, louder and longer than Nicole's joke called for.

When I finally stopped, I looked at her and smiled.

"Thank you for that," I said. "And for not pretending this doesn't suck."

Nicole clinked her glass against mine. "Always."

caleb

I'D JUST FINISHED routine maintenance when I heard it.

The Lochwell had a sound when it was running right—steady, even, almost invisible if you'd been around it long enough. This wasn't that sound. I'd been servicing this building for over ten years and knew whatever that whir was meant something was off.

It was a low, uneven grind under the usual hum, like something was working harder than it should be to keep up.

I walked down the mechanical corridor, listening. When I narrowed it down, I frowned.

"Yeah," I muttered. "That's not good."

I popped the panel and leaned in, flashlight cutting across familiar parts. The blower motor kicked on again, protesting louder this time, the vibration confirming what I already knew.

Worn bearings. Maybe worse.

I checked the amp draw, then the control board. Nothing catastrophic yet, but it was heading that way—

one hot week or one bad surge from turning into an emergency call no one wanted.

I straightened just as Carli came through the door, iPad tucked under her arm, clearly responding to the text I'd sent.

"What's up?"

"Nothing good," I said.

"Seriously?"

"Unfortunately."

"What's going on?"

"While I was finishing up maintenance, I heard a noise," I said. "Listen."

Carli stopped beside me, listening for a beat.

"Please tell me that noise isn't what I think it is," she said.

I snorted. "Depends on what you think it is."

"Expensive."

"Then yes."

She sighed, leaning against the wall. "How bad?"

"Not today bad.'" I tapped the panel with my knuckles. "But this unit's on borrowed time. We're getting to the point where repairs aren't worth the cost."

She grimaced. "Can you give me a timeline?"

I tilted my head, considering. "Could be six months. Or it could die on the hottest day of August when everyone's home and cranky."

"Of course it could," she said.

"If I were you, I'd start planning for a replacement now," I said. "You don't want to wait until it fails completely. Emergency installs cost more, and you'll have residents without AC while you scramble."

"I appreciate you staying on top of this," Carli said.

"Most people wouldn't have noticed anything was wrong yet."

"I've been listening to this building for a long time," I said as I finished up the work order on my tablet and had Carli sign it. "You know the drill...your copy will be emailed, and a salesperson will be in touch about your replacement options."

"Sounds good."

I packed my tools and slung the bag over my shoulder, then followed Carli out of the mechanical room. She veered off to put out her next fire while I headed down the hall to the small bathroom near the service stairs.

Thankfully, it had been an easy day. No crawlspaces, no blown motors, no sweat-soaked emergencies. I checked my reflection in the mirror as I scrubbed my hands up to my elbows, rinsing off the lingering grit until the water ran clear. After drying off, I dragged my fingers through my hair. My friends will just have to deal with my hat head. I was good enough for a drink at The Foundry.

I grabbed my bag and headed out to stash it in my truck. The air was warm but comfortable, the kind of May afternoon that made everything feel a little easier. I shut the tailgate with a solid thunk, then pulled out my phone to check the time. It was just about four. The guys wouldn't roll in until at least four-thirty. Normally, I'd kill the time walking the river path or looping the grounds around The Lochwell, letting my brain power down. But I wasn't in the mood for that today, so I headed straight to the pub.

Inside, The Foundry was in that sweet spot before the evening rush hit. There were people scattered at a few tables and '80s rock playing low in the background. I took a seat at the end of the bar.

"Hey, Caleb."

Elsie Rowe was working behind the bar. She graduated with my sister Nora, so we go way back.

"What can I get you?" she asked.

"Lochwell Lager."

I watched her pour a perfect pint, then slide it toward me before filling a bowl with popcorn and setting it on the bar.

"Where's Duncan tonight?" I asked.

"He's not feeling great, so he asked me to cover," she said. "How's Nora doing?"

"Good," I said. "Busy. Happy."

"Tell her I said hi. It feels like forever."

"I'll tell her to stop in next time she's in."

"That'd be great."

Someone approached the other end of the bar and she walked over to wait on them.

I took a long drink. The beer was crisp and cold and hit the spot. I chased it with a handful of popcorn, my eyes drifting to the wall behind the taps as I chewed. Framed black-and-white photos of Lochwell Brewing back when this place was still a working brewery filled the space. Men in suspenders standing in front of massive copper tanks. Women bottling by hand. The old delivery truck parked out front like it had nowhere else to be.

As sad as it is that the brewery closed, I was glad Duncan was willing to pivot. Most people would've clung to it out of pride. He'd built something different instead, an amazing community.

At least the beer survived. It was sold off to keep the rest of this place alive.

I took another drink just as the door opened. Elsie glanced toward the entrance, then briefly toward me. She tilted her head in that direction and scrunched her nose. I looked over my shoulder and saw Rachel standing in the doorway, sunglasses perched on top of her head, hair longer than the last time I'd seen her. She scanned the room, then her eyes landed on me.

She said something to her friends, then walked in my direction.

"Caleb," she said, smiling. "Hi."

"Hey," I said. "In town for a visit?"

"No, I actually moved back."

"Oh, I didn't know."

"Yeah, I've been here a couple weeks now."

I nodded, taking another sip of my beer. "How's it going?"

"Good," she said. Her gaze dropped—just briefly—to the logo stitched on my T-shirt. "Still working for Fletcher?"

"I am," I said.

"Wow." She let out a soft laugh. "It's been a long time."

I wasn't sure what to say to that, so I didn't respond.

She shifted her weight. "I heard you bought a house."

"Yeah."

"In Maplemoor?"

I took a drink and nodded. "Not far from my parents."

"Ah. On the compound."

"It's not a compound."

"That's what everyone in town calls it."

"It's just...a few blocks where most of my family ended up," I said.

"Uh-huh," she said with a smirk. "Sure."

She clearly meant to be funny, but her teasing still stung. She'd always talked about wanting a house near family. Then one day, she didn't want that at all.

She smiled again, but this one didn't quite reach her eyes. "You look good."

"Thanks. So do you."

There was a pause. Not uncomfortable. Just full.

"Well," she said eventually. "We should catch up sometime. Maybe grab dinner?"

The question hung between us.

A few years ago, I might have taken her up on her offer. Not now.

"I don't think that's a good idea," I said.

Her smile faltered. "Oh."

The silence stretched between us, awkward and weighted with history. Before I could ruin it by listing all the reasons getting together was a terrible idea, Mason walked up.

"Hey, Rachel."

She blinked at him, clearly searching for recognition. I couldn't blame her. The man standing in front of us—sharp haircut, tailored suit—barely resembled the long-haired, barefoot hippie she'd left behind.

"Hi, Mason," she said finally.

Not everything that broke should be repaired.

CHAPTER SEVEN

I'D HAD A LATE MEETING, so book club was in full swing by the time I got to The Brewhouse.

The high-top tables were pushed together like they always were, everyone already settled in with coffee cups, iced drinks, and the remains of whatever pastries had been deemed necessary tonight. Alexis and Tiff were mid-conversation, Ilona laughing at something Leeta had just said.

Maggie and Emily were talking about something that had happened at school that morning.

I grabbed a Book Club Blend at the counter before heading over, the mug warm against my palms.

"There she is," Tiff said as I set it down and slid onto the empty stool.

Emily turned to look at me. "About time."

"My meeting ran long," I said.

That wasn't a lie—it had. But I still could've been here on time if I'd left right after. Instead, I sat on my couch, staring at nothing, letting the minutes tick by.

Nicole's wedding was getting close enough that I could feel it.

I kept telling myself I'd be fine. I wasn't sure I believed it.

"We considered sending a rescue text," Alexis said.

I chuckled and took a sip of tea.

"So," she said easily. "How was the bachelorette weekend?"

"It was good," I said. "Really good."

"We're living vicariously here," Tiff said. "We need details."

"Nicole wanted a classy bachelorette, and that's pretty much what we delivered," I said. "We did some touristy stuff—walking along the river, poking into boutiques—but Sunday was a full spa day, which honestly might've been my favorite part. And then the last night we hired a personal chef to come in and cook a small-plates dinner, which felt like the perfect way to end the trip."

Alexis smiled. "I love Savannah. It's so chill down there."

"I've never been," Ilona said. "But that sounds exactly like my kind of trip."

"Same," Leeta said.

I nodded, wrapping my hands around my mug. "It really was nice. I highly recommend visiting if you get a chance."

The conversations scattered again, breaking into smaller threads around the table. I took a sip of my tea and listened, only half following along as my mind drifted back to Savannah—sitting with Nicole after everyone else had gone to bed, letting her talk while I kept my own thoughts tucked away.

Maggie's voice cut through it, gentle and steady. "You okay?"

I blinked, my focus snapping back to the table.

"Yeah," I said automatically. Her raised brow had me adding, "Mostly."

Maggie studied me for a second, then nodded. "Do you want to talk about it?"

The overlapping conversations around us tapered off. No one rushed me or filled the silence.

I took a breath and let it out slowly.

"Brett's engaged," I said.

Emily's head snapped up. "I'm sorry—what?"

Alexis swore softly under her breath. Tiff's mouth fell open.

"You're kidding," Ilona said.

"That's—." Leeta started, then stopped. "A lot."

I shook my head.

"Yeah, it was a shock for sure."

Maggie and Tiff spoke at the same time.

"How'd you find out?"

"When did you find out?"

"Last week, when Nicole called during book club."

Maggie studied me for a moment. "How are you feeling about it?"

"Honestly?" I shrugged. "Not great."

Ilona nodded. "Of course it doesn't feel great."

I took a breath. "I know I'm better off," I said, because that part mattered. "I really do. I love my life here and wouldn't trade any of it."

Maggie nodded, encouraging but quiet.

"But," I continued, fingers tightening around my mug, "we were together for more than a decade. When things started feeling like they were moving forward, he pulled back. Said he didn't want marriage. And now he's engaged." I held my hands out. "So I get it. It's not that he didn't want marriage. He just didn't want it with me."

"He's a dick," Tiff said flatly.

Emily snorted into her coffee.

Maggie shot her a look.

"What?" Tiff said. "He is."

"Well said," Maggie said.

Tiff shrugged and took a sip of her iced coffee.

A small laugh slipped out of me before I could stop it. That's why I love Tiff. She's brash, loyal, and absolutely the person I'd want beside me in a fight.

The moment settled again, quieter this time.

Maggie tilted her head. "Can I ask you something?"

"Sure."

"Why didn't you tell us?"

My hands tightened around the mug. "I didn't want to make it a thing." I glanced around the table. "You all have enough going on. I figured I could handle it."

"I hate that you felt like you had to hold that by your-self," Maggie said.

Tiff shook her head. "Next time, you say something. Even if it's awkward."

"That's what we're here for," Leeta said.

I stared down at the table, breathing through the sting behind my eyes.

The table stayed quiet, not heavy—just patient.

Leeta was the one who finally spoke. "That's kind of how this happened," she said. "The closeness, I mean."

I looked up. "How what happened?"

She shrugged. "People came and went over the years. But when we started meeting in person again, the ones who stayed...stayed. And kept showing up."

Maggie nodded once, subtle.

"It wasn't planned," Leeta continued. "There wasn't a moment where someone decided we were going to become this whole thing. It just happened."

Tiff snorted softly. "Turns out consistency is a personality trait."

A few smiles went around the table.

Leeta glanced at Maggie, then back at me. "When Maggie's husband died, that's when things shifted. The book club stopped being just books."

I hesitated, meeting Maggie's eyes. "I knew he passed, but I never asked what happened. I'm sorry."

"It was sudden. One day he was there. The next he wasn't."

Her words landed hard.

"At first, there were people everywhere," Maggie went on. "Food, texts, check-ins. Support is loud at the beginning." She paused. "Then it fades."

Leeta smiled at her. "But we kept showing up. Not as a book club. Just as people who weren't going anywhere."

A quiet huff of laughter escaped me before I could stop it.

They'd already decided I wasn't doing this by myself.

Something in my chest loosened, slow and unfamiliar.

Alexis's voice was gentle. "How are you holding up?"

I took a second before answering, choosing my words instead of letting them spill. I gave them the short version—the surprise, the sting, the part where I still wondered if I'd been too much.

Tiff leaned toward me. "That's ridiculous. You're fucking perfect."

My mouth curled into a small smile before I could stop it.

"The worst part," I said, "is that I'm going to have to see them at Nicole's wedding in a few weeks."

Emily tilted her head. "Then you definitely shouldn't go alone."

"It'll be okay," I added quickly. "I'll be too busy being the maid of honor to pay attention to them."

Tiff leaned back. "You need to bring a hot date."

I shook my head. "Hot or not, they know every single guy I'd even consider asking."

"What about someone local?" Alexis asked.

"You ladies are basically my social life in Maplemoor," I said with a chuckle. "I don't know any guys I'd feel comfortable asking to spend a whole weekend in Philadelphia with me."

Emily's smile made me nervous.

"I don't like that look."

"Jess," she said. "Hear me out."

"What?"

"What about Caleb?"

I blinked. "Caleb?"

Something shifted low in my stomach, which I immediately blamed on the coffee.

"Yes," she said, clearly pleased with herself. "Caleb."

"Oh, I love that idea," Alexis said.

Before I could say anything, Emily continued.

"He's single, you already know each other, and he can hold his own on the dance floor."

"And he's a good guy," Leeta said. "So you'd be safe spending the weekend with him."

Alexis leaned in. "And he cleans up well."

"And I'll personally make sure he gets a much-needed haircut," Emily said.

I looked around the table at them. "You're very confident about this."

"For good reason," Emily said.

I opened my mouth to argue.

Nothing came out.

"I don't hate that idea," I said carefully.

"Perfect," Emily said, already reaching for her phone.

"That's not a yes."

"Didn't say it was," she said cheerfully. "But it's close enough."

She tapped the screen.

"Emily—"

She lifted a finger at me, grinning as the phone started to ring.

caleb

MURPHY BARRELED ACROSS THE YARD, skidding to a stop at my feet like he expected applause. I laughed and tossed the ball again just as my phone buzzed in my pocket.

Emily.

I frowned at the screen. Emily never called. She texted —usually in complete sentences, occasionally with bullet points. A phone call meant something was wrong.

"Hey."

"Quick question for you."

"Dangerous way to start a conversation."

"You're not wrong, but hear me out."

"Okay," I said, drawing out the word as I scratched Murphy behind the ears.

"How do you feel about weddings?" she asked.

"That depends," I said. "Am I attending or escaping one?"

"Attending with a beautiful woman."

I paused.

"You know how I feel about setups."

"This isn't that," she said immediately.

"That's what you said last time."

"And this time I'm being very clear," she said. "This is not a setup. It's logistics."

"Logistics that involve going to a wedding with a beautiful woman," I said. "That feels like a gray area."

"It's really not," she insisted. "Jess is in the wedding."

Murphy wandered off and settled into his favorite corner of the deck, circling once before flopping down. I dragged my fingers through my hair.

"Okay."

"So is her ex."

I winced. "Still okay."

"And," she added, "he just got engaged."

"There's the punchline."

"She's handling it, but it would really suck for her to show up alone and look like she hasn't moved on."

"And you think I'm the solution."

"You already know each other. You're single. And you can hold your own on the dance floor."

I snorted. "You have a lot of confidence in me."

"For good reason," she said. "I know you'll behave."

"What's that supposed to mean?"

"It's in Philadelphia, so you'll be spending the weekend together," Emily said.

"Ah, the plot thickens."

"And I know you'll be a perfect gentleman."

"Does Jess know you called me?"

"Yeah, she's right here."

"Right here as in—"

"Book club," she said. "at The Brewhouse."

That gave me a moment of pause—not because Jess was there, but because I'd assumed this conversation was happening away from her. Talking about someone while they sat ten feet away felt wrong.

And then there was the rest of it.

I pictured Rachel. A wedding a few months after we broke up would've been bad enough. Seeing her there, newly engaged, would've been worse. Yeah. I got why this mattered.

"You should come down and talk with her," Emily said. "Get the details straight from the source instead of me playing middleman."

I glanced at Murphy, still sprawled in his favorite corner of the deck, then back toward the house.

"Give me fifteen minutes," I said.

"You're predictable in the best way."

I laughed despite myself. "I'm hanging up."

Still smiling, I slid my phone back into my pocket and whistled softly.

"Come on, Murph," I said. "I've gotta go out."

Fifteen minutes later, I was walking through the door to The Brewhouse.

The high-top tables were pushed together like they always were for book club. The conversation didn't stop when I walked in, but it softened.

Emily looked at me, her expression far too satisfied.

Jess sat near the middle of the table, hands wrapped around a mug. She didn't look up right away. When she did, her mouth curved like she wasn't sure whether to smile or apologize.

"Perfect timing," Emily said as she pushed out the chair between her and Jess.

Instead of sitting, I rested my forearms on the back of it and leaned forward.

"Hey," I said to Jess.

"Hi."

Emily gestured between us. "Jess, why don't you fill Caleb in on the basics?"

"Let's head outside so we can talk in private," I said before Jess could speak, directing the last two words at my sister.

"Oh," Jess said, then nodded. "Sure."

She stood, and I followed her out to the patio, where she automatically headed for an empty table near the railing. As I sat across from her, I caught the book club watching us through the window. I ignored them and focused on Jess, where my attention belonged.

"Before we talk about the wedding," I said, "I just want to make sure this is something you actually want. Not something Emily decided on your behalf."

"I wouldn't have agreed if I didn't want to." She flashed a wry smile. "I just might not have thought of it on my own."

"Okay, tell me about the wedding."

"It's in Philadelphia. The rehearsal is Friday night, the wedding is Saturday, and there's a brunch Sunday morning."

"Emily said you're in the wedding."

She nodded. "I'm the maid of honor."

"So it's not exactly something you can bow out of."

"Nope," she said, popping the P. "And honestly, I was resigned to seeing my ex there, but now..."

"Emily said he got engaged."

"Yeah, I found out last week."

I glanced toward the window, where the book club was doing a very poor job of pretending not to watch us, then back to Jess.

"Okay. Then if we're doing this, we probably shouldn't walk into that wedding acting like strangers."

"What do you mean?"

"We should probably spend some time together before then," I said. "So we don't look like we met in the parking lot."

She chuckled. "Like...practice?"

"More like coffee. Dinners. Hikes. Normal human interaction."

She glanced at me, studying my face like she was checking for something. Judgment, maybe. Or pity.

All I felt was a steady, grounded understanding.

"You're sure about this?"

"Positive."

"I'm not looking for anything dramatic. You don't have to act like you're madly in love with me or anything," she said. "I just don't want to spend the whole weekend feeling like a sad footnote."

"I get that," I said. "And why don't we just play it by ear once we're there?"

"Thank you." She reached out and squeezed my hand. "Really."

"You're welcome."

Her smile lingered this time.

And for the first time since my conversation with Emily, the situation didn't feel like a favor.

It felt like a choice.

CHAPTER NINE

I WATCHED Caleb head down the sidewalk, hands in his pockets, like agreeing to be my wedding date hadn't been a big deal.

Except it was.

Sitting there, I realized I felt lighter than I had since Nicole told me about Brett's engagement. I hadn't even realized how tense I'd been until it eased.

I took in a deep breath, let it out slowly, and stood. The women inside deserved an update.

"Well?" Tiff said, as soon as I walked in the door.

I slid back into my seat and shook my head once, mostly to stop myself from smiling. "He's going."

Emily's grin was instant. Alexis made a delighted noise that sounded suspiciously like a squeal. Ilona clapped her hands together, and Leeta's smile was quieter but just as satisfied. Maggie just watched me for a moment, then nodded, like she'd known what would happen.

"I told you," Emily said, lifting her coffee like she was toasting her own brilliance.

"You absolutely did not," I chuckled. "You basically ambushed him."

"She facilitated," Maggie said calmly.

"Thank you," Emily said.

Tiff leaned forward, eyes bright. "Okay, but like... actually going? Or did he say yes in that polite, noncommittal way men sometimes do?"

Once I confirmed Caleb was officially going with me, the table buzzed again—easier this time.

"Okay," Alexis said, leaning in. "Do you have a picture of your bridesmaid dress?"

"I do." I scrolled through my phone until I found it, then turned the screen toward the girls. "This is from my last fitting."

"Oh, I love that," Ilona said immediately.

"The sage is perfect on you," Maggie said. "And not something you'll hate every time you see it in photos."

"That was the goal," I said. "Nicole wanted something that felt timeless without screaming bridal party."

Emily squinted at the screen. "Turn it back. I want to see the neckline again."

I did, and she nodded approvingly. "Very flattering."

"And it's comfortable," I said. "Which is important, considering how long the day's going to be."

Leeta smiled. "You look really good, Jess."

Something in her tone made my chest warm a little. "Thanks."

"What about your hair?" Tiff asked. "Up or down?"

"Up," I said. "We're all doing some kind of updo. Nicole hired a stylist to come to the hotel the morning of the wedding and work her magic. She also has a makeup artist coming, so I don't have to worry about that either."

"Perfect," Leeta said. "No stress. Just show up and sit."

"That's the plan," I said. "But I still have to decide what I'm wearing to the rehearsal. I have three options in mind." I smiled. "I do have my shoes picked out, though."

"Tell us about them," Alexis said with a little flutter-clap.

"They're champagne metallic Jimmy Choo Azia sandals."

"My heart literally just skipped a beat," she said. "I love shoes. And I used to wear heels every day pre-kids. Now it's flip-flops, sneakers, or boots. So I'll live vicariously through you."

"Heels aren't my usual footwear, but I splurged and bought them when I got my first big-girl job. I've only worn them once, though." I smiled. "At least I won't have to worry about wearing them to the wedding with Caleb."

Emily frowned slightly. "Why?"

"Because Caleb's tall."

They all stared at me for a beat.

"And?" Ilona prompted.

I shrugged. "Brett's only an inch or two taller than me and hated when I wore heels. Said it made him 'feel weird.'" I made air quotes with my fingers. "So I usually wore flats around him."

There was a collective pause.

"Oh," Emily said flatly. "So we're dealing with a short-man complex."

"He's not short. I'm just tall," I said automatically, then shrugged. "And he hated when I towered over him."

Tiff snorted. "That makes this even better."

"How?" I asked.

"Because," Emily said, clearly enjoying herself, "you're showing up with a six-five guy in a tailored suit. That's going to absolutely ruin your ex."

I couldn't help but laugh at the thought of that. "That's not the goal."

"Sure it is," Tiff said.

"No," I said, smiling but firm. "My goal is to get through the weekend without losing my mind. Anything else is just...a bonus."

Emily smirked at me like she didn't believe that for a second.

The conversation flowed easily from there, drifting to their own weddings, to getting dressed up just to go out, and the kinds of nights that felt huge at the time and smaller in hindsight. No pressure. No intensity. Just women who'd done this before, who knew how to make it feel manageable instead of overwhelming.

And for the first time since Savannah, the idea of the wedding didn't feel like something I had to brace myself for.

When book club finally wound down, I said my good-byes and stepped back out into the night. The walk home was short and familiar, the kind of quiet Maplemoor evening that made everything feel a little softer around the edges.

I kicked off my shoes as I walked through the door, tossing my purse onto the chair by the door. The scent of vanilla from the candle I'd had burning earlier hung in the air.

Candles had been one of the first things I claimed after Brett and I broke up. He'd hated anything "smelly," so I never used them when we lived together. Now I burned them whenever I was home, like a quiet reminder that this space was mine.

I sank onto the couch and pulled my phone from my

bag, hovering over Nicole's name for a second before typing.

> Hey. Can I add a plus-one?

Her reply came almost instantly.

> YES!!! Why?

I smiled and typed back.

> Because I have a date.

Three dots appeared. Disappeared. Appeared again. Then my phone rang.

I laughed under my breath and answered. "Hi."

"Okay," Nicole said, skipping right past hello. "First of all, I love that for you. Second of all, tell me everything."

"Before you start planning our wedding, he's not a date-date. More like an emotional support date so I don't have to sit alone while my ex parades his new life around."

"Uh-huh," Nicole said. "That's exactly what everyone says right before they accidentally bring a very hot man into the mix."

Caleb's face flashed through my mind. Brown hair, strong jaw, eyes that shifted between green and hazel and tended to be distracting either way.

I pushed the thought aside.

"He's a very nice man who agreed to accompany me to your wedding," I said. "That's it."

"If anyone asks me, I'll say that with a wink."

"Please don't," I said dryly.

Her laugh echoed through the phone.

"Okay," I said, shifting on the couch. "I need to get online and book a room for Caleb."

"Maybe Caleb won't want his own room."

I rolled my eyes, even though she couldn't see me.

"I'll talk to you later."

"I can't wait," Nicole said. "Love you."

"Love you, too."

I disconnected the call and reached for my laptop. After pulling up the hotel website, I keyed in the dates. No availability.

Seriously?

After refreshing the page, I got the same result.

Grabbing my phone, I typed in the number listed and pressed 2 for reservations.

A cheerful voice answered after two rings.

"Reservations, how can I help you?"

"Hi, I'm part of the Anderson-Matthews wedding and I need to book a room for Friday through Sunday."

There was a pause, keys clicking softly in the background.

"I'm sorry," she said. "That hotel is completely booked that weekend."

"Completely?"

"Yes, ma'am. We're fully sold out that weekend," she said. "If you'd like, I can put you on the waitlist."

"That would be great," I said and gave her my information.

I hung up and rested my head against the back of the couch.

The laptop screen still glowed in front of me, the words *No Availability* smugly staring back at me. After a beat, I straightened again and searched first the hotels in walking distance, then a few blocks out.

They're either fully booked or way out of my price range. Downtown Philadelphia is not cheap.

I took in a deep breath and let it out slowly.

Well, that complicates things.

Sharing a room with a man I barely knew was one thing. Sharing a room with a man whose jaw I'd apparently been cataloguing was another.

Caleb had agreed to accompany me to a wedding, not have a slumber party.

I grabbed my phone and texted Nicole.

Minor problem…the hotel is totally booked.

Her reply came fast.

Oh, no.

Then another.

Guess you and your guy are sharing.

I snorted. It's amazing how seven words could convey so much snark.

If he's still willing to go with me.

caleb

I BALANCED on a ladder in The Lochwell's mechanical room, one arm braced against the wall while I adjusted a damper, when my phone buzzed in my pocket.

I ignored it.

The unit cycled again, airflow uneven, just enough to confirm my suspicion. I made a small adjustment, listened, then tightened the screw and waited through another cycle. Better. Not perfect, but better.

The phone buzzed again, reminding me I hadn't checked it.

I closed the panel, climbed down, and washed my hands in the utility sink. After filling out a work order, I reached into my pocket and pulled out my phone.

Jess.

Seeing her name on my screen felt...unexpected. Not unwelcome. Just unexpected.

Hey. Vee mentioned you're working in the building today. I'm at The Brewhouse—any chance you could stop down if you have a minute?

I read it once. Then again.

Straightforward. Polite. Very Jess.

I leaned back against the wall, the low hum of the unit steady behind me. Maybe she was having second thoughts.

It wouldn't be unreasonable. She'd asked me to go away with her for a weekend, not pick up groceries. People were allowed to wake up and rethink things. I'd done it myself more than once.

I checked the time to make sure I had a window. Enough for coffee. Enough for a conversation that might end with never mind.

> Yeah. I can swing down in a few minutes.

Her reply came almost immediately.

> That'd be great. Thanks.

No emoji. No exclamation point. Which somehow made it harder to read, not easier.

I slipped the phone back into my pocket, then folded the ladder and packed up my tools. After making sure the mechanical room was in order, I walked out and headed for the service stairs.

My boots echoed softly against the concrete stairs as I made my way up to ground level. The basement smelled faintly industrial—oil, dust, and slightly musty—but by the time I pushed through the side door, that gave way to coffee and something sweet baking.

After stowing my ladder and tools in the truck, I headed across the courtyard toward The Brewhouse. It was pretty crowded for midday on a Thursday. Most of the tables were occupied by single people hunched over laptops, including the one Jess had claimed. She already had a scone and a coffee beside her, so I took my place in line, ordered an iced tea and a sandwich, and waited it out before threading my way over to her table.

She looked up as I approached.

"Hey," she said. "Thanks for stopping in."

"Sure." I settled into the chair across from her, opened my chips, and popped one into my mouth. "What's up?"

Her index finger tapped against the table while she nibbled her bottom lip. I figured she'd get to the reason she asked me to come eventually. I took a bite of my sandwich and chewed as I waited. The way she was avoiding looking at me made me wonder if she was about to tell me she'd changed her mind.

"So," she said, her eyes everywhere but on me. "I wanted to talk to you."

I took a sip of iced tea, attention still on her, waiting.

"I ran into a small complication last night." She finally looked at me. "The hotel is completely booked."

I blinked once.

"I looked online. I called. I even tried nearby hotels," she said, ticking them off on her fingers. "Everything was either full or insanely expensive."

Silence stretched between us as she watched my face like she was bracing for something.

"Okay," I said, resting my forearms on the table. "So there are no rooms at the hotel."

She nodded.

"What about somewhere outside the city? We could drive in," I said. "It wouldn't be ideal, but it's doable."

Her fingers curled tighter around her coffee cup.

"I have a room," she said. "I just couldn't get a second one for you."

"Oh, that's...workable. If you're okay with it."

Her brows knit together.

"You're sure?"

"Positive," I said, a small smile tugging at my mouth. "Besides," I added, "it kind of helps the fake dating story."

She blinked at me, then let out a small, incredulous laugh.

"You're still willing to go with me?"

"Yes."

After a few beats, her shoulders dropped a fraction. Relief, plain and unguarded.

"Thank you," she said quietly.

"You don't have to thank me."

"I kind of do."

She lifted her coffee, like she needed something to do with her hands. I watched her take a sip, The Brewhouse noise filling in the spaces neither of us rushed to occupy.

My gaze drifted to her laptop, and I tipped my head toward it.

"Please tell me you're not writing another proposal for some pain-in-the-ass building."

"Different building," she said with a smile. "Same personality."

"Historic?"

"Of course," she said.

I huffed a quiet laugh. "Shocking."

She relaxed a little then, shoulders easing, the tension that had been holding her together loosening just enough to make the moment feel...normal. Like this wasn't a high-stakes conversation that could've gone sideways ten minutes ago.

I finished my sandwich, then wiped my hands on a napkin as I chewed.

"So, now that we're done with wedding logistics—" I paused, then tipped my head toward her. "—we talked about spending some time together to get to know each other better." She nodded. "There's a trail just outside town," I said. "Nothing intense. Murphy loves it because you pass a waterfall."

"That sounds nice."

"Are you free this weekend to go?"

"I'd love to." She smiled. "Murphy's coming, right?"

"If you want him to."

"I do."

"Okay then. Let's plan for Saturday morning around ten?"

"That's perfect."

"I should get back to work." I finished my drink then tucked my garbage into the bag. "The coils at the hospital aren't going to clean themselves."

"Sounds fun."

"It's a dirty job, but someone's gotta do it," I said and stood. "But at least it's at the end of the day so I can go home right after and shower and change."

"Nothing better than finishing a gross job and knowing you get to be done for the day."

"Exactly," I said. "So I'll meet you here Saturday morning at ten?"

"I'll be here."

"Great. We can grab a bite then hit the road."

"Can't wait."

I walked over to toss my trash in the can. Before I headed toward the door, Jess called my name.

"Just so you know, you don't have to worry," she said as I approached the table again. "The room has two beds."

"I wasn't worried."

Her answering smile was softer, more relaxed.

I stepped back from the table, shifting my weight, halfway to leaving then paused.

"Hey," I said, turning back to her. "Can you do me a favor?"

"Yeah?"

I leaned in slightly, lowering my voice like we were conspiring.

"Don't tell Emily about this."

CHAPTER ELEVEN

MURPHY PAUSED near a bend in the trail and looked back, his ears lifting slightly.

Caleb glanced down at him. "Go ahead."

That was all it took.

He ran ahead, weaving easily through sunlit patches cast by the new leaves overhead, the light flashing briefly across his black fur. The way he moved—confident, unhurried—made it obvious this trail wasn't new to him.

At a curve in the path, Murphy stopped and turned back to look at us, his tail wagging.

Caleb didn't raise his voice. He didn't even break stride.

"Okay," he said.

Murphy turned and ran on, disappearing around the bend before slowing again, never far enough that we lost sight of him.

I smiled. "He listens so well."

"I can't really take credit for that," Caleb said. "He came that way."

I glanced at him. "Really?"

"He was already like this when I adopted him."

"How old was he?"

"About a year," he said. "There was an adoption event at the courthouse. I was walking through town and figured I'd take a look."

"And?"

He huffed a quiet laugh. "Every time I tried to walk away from him, he barked at me. The volunteer finally said, 'I think he's picked you.'"

"That's so sweet," I said.

"I hesitated at first."

"Why?"

"My schedule's all over the place. I didn't think it was fair to bring a dog home if I couldn't give him enough time." Caleb looked at the dog, then back at the trail. "One of the volunteers told me whatever time I could give him was still better than sending him back to a kennel." He paused. "I didn't really have an argument for that."

"So you just...did it?" I asked.

He nodded. "Filled out the paperwork right there. Picked him up a couple days later."

Murphy trotted back toward us, brushing against Caleb's leg before taking off again.

"Best decision I've ever made," he added.

I glanced at him. "You're as nice as they say you are."

The corner of his mouth lifted. "Who says?"

"The book club ladies," I said, then shrugged. "They wouldn't suggest you go to the wedding with me if it wasn't true."

"That's a pretty solid endorsement."

Caleb fell into step beside me, his attention drifting ahead to where Murphy had paused again on the trail.

It was quiet in the way good places usually are—not silent, just muted. Sunlight cut through the sparse leaves overhead, striping the path in warm, uneven patches. Only the crunch of gravel underfoot and the faint jingle of Murphy's tags filled the space.

"Okay, tell me what I need to know about the wedding."

My stomach tightened for a split second—my brain jumping to things I wasn't ready to unpack—before I caught myself.

"What do you want to know?"

"Dress code," he said. "Suit or tux?"

"Suit's fine," I said. "Formal, but not black-tie."

He nodded. "And timeline?"

"The rehearsal's at six, with dinner right after," I said. "What time do you think you could be ready to head out?"

"I figured I'd work a half day," he said. "Be ready to hit the road by noon."

"You don't have to do that."

"I know," he said. "But I want to."

I looked at him for a beat, then nodded and turned my attention back to the path.

"So if we leave around noon," I said, "giving time for traffic, we should be in Philly by three."

"That works," he said.

"Saturday morning I'll be tied up with the bridal party—hair, makeup, all of that."

"So I'm on my own for a bit."

"Yeah," I said. "You're officially off duty then."

The corner of his mouth lifted. "Good to know."

"Ceremony and reception are at the same place later that afternoon," I added. "I'll disappear again for photos, but once things get going, we'll mostly be together."

I hadn't realized how much I'd been bracing myself until just now.

"Okay."

"And there's brunch Sunday at eleven," I said. "We can head out right after."

"How do you want us to look?" he asked. "In front of people, I mean."

"Nothing over the top," I said. "Just...together."

"That works."

Somewhere ahead, water moved over stone. I couldn't see it yet, but I could hear the steady, constant flow, like a marker pulling us forward.

Murphy clearly knew where we were headed. He picked up speed, stopping less often now, his tail wagging higher as he darted ahead and doubled back, impatient but never too far away.

"Looks like he knows where he's going."

"He remembers this spot," I said.

We walked for a few minutes without talking, the kind of silence that didn't feel like it needed filling. I focused on my breathing, on the rhythm of my steps lining up without effort.

The trees thinned as the path opened onto a wide, flat stretch of rock. The waterfall spilled down the stone face ahead of us, not massive but persistent, water catching the sunlight as it fanned out and disappeared into a shallow pool below.

Murphy reached it first, skidding to a stop at the edge and barking once, sharp and proud, like he'd personally led us to something worth seeing.

"Okay, that's pretty great," I said, as I took in the sight.

"It is." He nodded toward the trees. "This is one of my favorites."

We stood there for a moment, side by side, watching the water flow over the rocks and settle into the crystal pool below. Murphy lowered his head and took three enthusiastic gulps of water, then paused and, without warning, launched himself straight into the shallow pool.

Caleb winced, then shook his head.

"Guess someone is getting a bath when we get home."

Water splashed everywhere as Murphy paddled in an uncoordinated circle before scrambling back out, tail whipping, coat already dark and slick. He walked toward us and shook, sending a fine mist of water in every direction.

I jumped back, laughing. "He looks very pleased with himself."

"He always is," Caleb said. "And if I don't wash him, he's going to smell like pond water for the next week."

Murphy trotted over and flopped down on the sun-warmed rock like none of this concerned him in the slightest.

"Zero remorse," I said.

"None," Caleb agreed.

I nodded in Murphy's direction. "Should we join him?"

Caleb gestured toward some flat rocks. "After you."

I found a spot and sat, bracing my hands behind me as I took in the steady fall of water. Caleb joined me, leaving a comfortable stretch of space between us. For a while, neither of us said anything. It didn't feel awkward. Just . . . settled. I watched Murphy doze, his chin on his paws, already drying in the sun. He let out a contented huff, but didn't bother opening his eyes.

For a few minutes, we just listened to the sounds of nature.

"Thank you," I said. "For doing this. For going with me."

He turned slightly, giving me his full attention, but didn't rush to respond.

"I was prepared to handle it on my own. The wedding.

Seeing them. All of it." I exhaled. "But it's . . . nice. Not having to."

A beat passed.

"I'm glad I can be there," he said.

The words settled in easily. No pressure. No expectation. Just presence.

And somehow, without me deciding it ahead of time, the whole thing felt more manageable.

caleb

BY THE TIME I walked up the path to Emily's house, Sunday dinner was in full swing. From inside came the layered noise of a baseball game, kids yelling, and what sounded like a pan hitting the counter a little harder than necessary.

I entered and sidestepped just in time to dodge a Nerf dart.

"Sorry, Uncle Caleb!" Danny yelled as he sprinted past me, plastic blaster in hand.

Christian barreled after him with a battle cry.

A dart bounced off my shoulder and landed near the entry table.

"Indoor voices," Haley called from somewhere deeper in the house, in the exact tone that meant she'd said it at least three times already.

Instead of walking straight into what I knew would be chaos in the kitchen, I followed the sound of the game into the living room.

Luke was on the couch with Teddy, both of them

leaning forward, eyes locked on the screen. The Lagerheads were up by one in the bottom of the third.

Dad sat in the recliner, remote in hand, like letting go might somehow cost them the lead.

"That was outside," Luke argued at the screen as Kofi Mensah went down looking.

Dad didn't look away. "Too close to take."

Luke was half off the couch, hands braced on his knees.

"Come on," he muttered at the screen.

I stayed near the doorway, shoulder against the frame, watching over their heads.

Cody Mitchell stepped into the box. Two on. Two out. The pitch came in and the crack of the bat cut through the room.

Luke shot to his feet. "That's gone."

The ball carried deep to left.

Without thinking, I pushed off the doorframe, stepping farther into the room.

"Stay fair," Luke barked.

It hooked just inside the foul pole for a three-run shot.

Teddy whooped. Dad gave a single, satisfied nod.

Luke threw both hands in the air. "Yes!"

He turned to say something to Teddy and finally noticed me standing there.

"Oh. You're here."

"Apparently," I said.

Luke jerked his chin toward the screen. "You see that?"

"Hard to miss."

On screen, the replay rolled for the third time. Then the camera switched to Mitchell tipping his hat to the crowd.

"Dinner's ready," Emily called from the dining room.

Luke leaned forward. "The inning isn't over."

Teddy nodded in solemn agreement.

On screen, the pitcher toed the rubber again.

Dad shifted in his chair. "You can record it."

Luke didn't look at him. "It's not the same."

"It's exactly the same if you don't know what happened," Dad said calmly.

Mom's voice cut through the house. "Now."

Dad sighed once and shut the TV off.

"We don't want to make her say it twice."

Luke groaned. "Unbelievable."

"You'll survive," Dad replied as he stood and stepped around the coffee table, remote still in hand.

Luke dragged himself up off the couch and Teddy followed.

I walked behind them toward the dining room, nudging a stray Nerf dart out of the way with my foot.

Emily set a pan of lasagna on the table and looked up at me. "Oh, good. You made it."

"Work wrapped early," I said.

"Miracles happen," she muttered.

Mom set two baskets of garlic bread down and inspected me like I hadn't just seen her forty-eight hours ago.

"You shave?" she asked.

"No."

She wrinkled her nose.

I hadn't seen the need to shave for a Sunday morning emergency call. Or dinner with my family.

That concluded her inspection.

By the time the noise settled into chairs scraping and silverware clinking, every plate had an identically sized square of lasagna. Emily cut like she was trying to impress a geometry teacher.

I reached for a slice of garlic bread before it disappeared.

Mom passed the salad she always insisted on making. It made the full trip around the table untouched. No one in this family was choosing rabbit food over lasagna.

Conversation layered over itself—school, work, Dad complaining about gas prices—until it blended into a steady hum.

I was halfway through my lasagna when Emily glanced up from her plate and squinted at me.

"I hope you're planning to get a haircut before the wedding."

Mom's head snapped up immediately. "What wedding?"

I glared at Emily.

"What wedding?" Mom asked again, holding a forkful of lasagna in midair.

Emily didn't even try to hide the smile tugging at her mouth.

I held her stare.

Luke leaned back in his chair, already entertained. "Oh, this should be good."

Mom turned fully toward me now. "You're going to a wedding?"

"Don't get too excited," I said evenly. "I'm just helping someone out."

"Helping," Emily repeated, like it required quotation marks.

Haley hid a grin.

"Are you *helping* anyone I know?"

"Jess Harper."

"From book club." Emily smirked at me over the rim of her glass.

I shot her a look. She smiled wider.

Mom's expression shifted into something I'd learned to

fear. "Will I get to see you two all dressed up before you leave?"

"It's a wedding," I said. "Not prom."

Luke barked out a laugh. "Not prom," he repeated.

"Besides," Emily said sweetly. "It's in Philadelphia."

Mom set her fork down. "You're going away for the weekend to a wedding to *help* someone?"

"Yeah," I said, like it wasn't complicated. "She needed a plus-one."

Luke muttered something about a "hero complex" around a mouthful of garlic bread.

Haley elbowed him without looking up.

Mom leaned back slightly, studying me the way she used to when I came home from a keg party in high school.

"Well," she said carefully, "that's very nice of you."

She looked at me another second, then nodded like she was letting it go. I knew better.

Mom wouldn't stop worrying about me until I was "settled," which, in her mind, meant married. Preferably with children.

Conversation shifted again—Teddy arguing about batting averages, Anna announcing she hated ricotta, someone asking for more garlic bread.

Normal. Loud. Familiar.

By the time we were pushing back from the table, I'd almost forgotten the interrogation.

Mom caught me near the sink while I stacked plates.

"You're going to get a haircut before you go," she said, not asking.

I glanced at her. "I'll handle it."

I'd probably wait until the last possible minute, just to keep them guessing.

CHAPTER THIRTEEN

MY MOM'S face appeared on my screen a second after I clicked connect.

She looked exactly the way she always does when we talk during the week—glasses on, hair up in a scrunchie, face freshly washed. It was only five here, but ten in Edinburgh.

"Hi," she said.

"Hi."

We both adjusted our laptops automatically, not because anything was wrong, just habit.

Normally my dad would drift into the corner of the screen at some point, hovering just inside the frame like he didn't want to fully commit to being on camera but also didn't want to miss anything.

Tonight it was just her.

"Dad's still in London?" I asked.

"Yeah, he'll be back Wednesday," she said. "It's been quiet without him."

She paused, then added with a small chuckle, "Which is sometimes nice."

I smiled.

Their apartment in Edinburgh wasn't small by European standards, but compared to the houses we'd rented when I was growing up, it felt compact. The kind of place where you always knew what room the other person was in.

The adjustment had taken them a minute.

But they'd adjusted...mostly.

"What are you doing with all the peace and quiet?" I asked.

"Working," she said immediately. "I'm trying to get ahead on edits before he gets back. I picked up two new clients."

"Overachiever."

"I'm freelance. If I don't overachieve, I don't get paid."

"Still on crime novels?"

"Yes. And I'm officially banning the phrase 'he ran a hand through his hair.'"

"Bold."

"I have standards."

She moved from the chair to the couch and adjusted the screen so I could see her again. "I did go out with the ladies last night, though."

"Oh, yeah? What'd you do?"

"Went to the pub. It was karaoke."

"What did you sing?"

"How do you know I sang?"

I rolled my eyes. "Seriously?"

She chuckled then took in a breath and let it out on a sigh.

"I wanted to do 'Edge of Seventeen,' but someone beat me to it."

"That's rude."

"Right?" she said. "So I had to pivot and sing 'Hit Me With Your Best Shot' by Pat Benatar."

"Another classic."

"One of my favorites." Her smile softened. "You seem less stressed than you did the other day."

"Yeah, I think I was more stressed about seeing Brett at the wedding than I realized," I admitted.

Her expression softened. "That makes sense."

"I kept telling myself it didn't matter," I said. "And it doesn't, in the big picture. I don't miss him or sitting around wishing things were different. But the idea of walking into that room and seeing him with his fiancée..." I exhaled. "It got in my head."

"And now it's not?" she asked gently.

I hesitated.

"Now I'm not going alone."

Her eyebrows lifted slightly.

"My friend Emily's brother Caleb offered to go with me," I said. "She basically volunteered him."

"And you're comfortable with that?"

"Yes, Mom," I said, smiling a little. "I am."

"How well do you know this Caleb?"

"I know him from around town. I mean—we're not strangers."

She held my gaze for a second. "And you feel comfortable going to Philadelphia for a weekend with him?"

"Yes," I said immediately.

"You're sure?"

"I wouldn't take him if I wasn't."

She held my gaze for a second, then nodded.

"Okay."

"I'm meeting him for dinner tonight," I added. "We

figured we should actually spend time together before the wedding so we don't look like we met in the parking lot."

"Smart," she said. "What's his last name?"

"Ward," I said. "Why?"

"So I can run a background check."

"*Mom.*"

"Just kidding." She chuckled. "You've always had a good head on your shoulders. I trust you."

"Besides, we don't need one," I said. "The book club vouched for him."

"Oh," she said. "Well it doesn't get better than that."

I laughed. "Exactly."

She shook her head, smiling—that familiar half-smile that means she thinks I'm ridiculous but also knows I'll be fine.

For a second it was easy.

I glanced briefly toward the window behind my laptop, the light outside already softening into evening, then looked back at her.

"I'm glad he's coming with me," I said. "I really didn't want to walk in there alone."

Her smile faded into something quieter. Not worried. Just listening.

"It's not that I want Brett back," I said, holding her gaze. "I don't. It just feels...humiliating. We were together for eleven years, and he's engaged after a few months."

"That's not humiliation," she said gently. "That's comparison."

"It doesn't feel that tidy."

"It never does," she said. "But it doesn't mean you did anything wrong. It just means that relationship ran its course. You're not behind because he rushed ahead."

I let out a small laugh. "Tell that to my nervous system."

She smiled faintly. "Your nervous system doesn't get to run the narrative."

"I know I'm better off without him," I said. "I really do. We weren't right at the end. I can see that now."

"And that's growth."

"I just didn't want to stand there alone while he looked...settled."

"And now you won't," she said simply.

"Yeah," I said. "I guess I won't."

She had a way of straightening out my thinking without making it a big deal.

"I should get going," I said. "It's nice out so I'm going to walk."

"Have a nice time," she said, that small, knowing smile tugging at her mouth.

"It's just dinner," I warned.

"I didn't say it wasn't," she replied.

"*Mom.*"

She laughed softly. "Go. Enjoy yourself."

"I will."

We said our goodbyes, and the screen went dark.

For a second, I sat there in the quiet of my apartment.

I pushed back from my desk, grabbed my coat from the hook by the door, and stepped outside.

The evening air was cool but not cold, the sky fading into that soft blue that only lasts a few minutes before night settles in. Maplemoor was already shifting into its after-work rhythm. It felt...steady.

I tucked my hands into my pockets and started toward Il Tavola di Maria.

caleb

JESS WALKED in a minute after I sat down.

"Hey," she said as she slipped out of her coat. "I hope you weren't waiting long."

"No. Just sat down."

"Good." She slid into the chair across from me. "I was on FaceTime with my mom and lost track of time."

The server appeared beside the table, setting down two glasses of water.

"Good evening," she said. "Can I bring you something else to drink while you look over the menu?"

She looked at Jess.

"I'll have a glass of red," Jess said. "Something dry."

"Our Nero d'Avola is very nice."

"That's perfect."

She glanced at me.

"And for you?"

"I'll take a Lochwell Summer Ale," I said.

After promising to bring them right over, she stepped away, leaving us alone.

I reached for my water.

"Your mom doing okay?"

She frowned slightly. "Yeah. Why?"

"You said you were on FaceTime."

"It was just our usual weekly call."

"Weekly?" I asked.

"Couple times a week, actually. The time difference makes it interesting."

"Time difference?"

A small smile tugged at her mouth.

"My parents live in Scotland."

"Scotland?"

She nodded. "Edinburgh. They moved there for my dad's job a few years ago."

The server returned with our drinks.

"Can I answer any questions about the menu?" she asked.

Jess shook her head. "I think I'm ready."

We ordered—she went with the cacio e pepe, I got the short rib ragu—and once the server stepped away again, I looked back at her.

"I just realized I don't actually know where you're from."

She let out a laugh. "That depends on how you define *from*."

"What's *your* definition?"

"I was born in Connecticut, but we moved every couple of years for my dad's work. I was basically an army brat without the military."

"Any siblings?" I asked, then took a sip of beer.

"Nope. Only child."

"I'm one of four. And I've lived in Maplemoor my whole life."

"That must've been nice."

"It was loud. Chaotic." I huffed a quiet laugh. "But yeah, it was nice."

Jess took a sip of her wine and glanced around the room.

"It's really cozy in here."

"You've never eaten here?"

"No," she said as she set her glass down and wrapped her fingers around the stem. "There's so much going on at The Lochwell, it's easy to forget there's an entire town outside of it."

I lifted my beer. "Then we'll consider this the beginning of expanding your Maplemoor radius."

A smile tugged at her mouth. She clinked her glass gently against mine. "Careful. I might start expecting guided tours."

The server came back a few minutes later with two wide bowls, steam curling up from both.

Jess's cacio e pepe looked simple but serious. Thick pasta twisted together, mixed with butter and cheese, cracked black pepper scattered over the top. It smelled sharp and salty in a way that made your mouth water.

Mine was heavier. Thick pieces of short rib were mixed through the pasta, not shredded down to nothing but left in solid, tender bites. The sauce clung to everything—dark red, almost brown at the edges like it had been simmering all day.

Jess leaned in over her bowl, eyes closed, and drew in a slow breath.

"Okay," she said, opening them again. "This smells amazing."

She twirled her fork, took a bite, and closed her eyes again as she chewed. I reached for my beer. She ate like no one was watching, which, given that I was, kind of felt like a moment.

"This is better than pasta I've had in Italy."

I huffed a quiet laugh. "The owner would expect nothing less."

Her brows lifted as she paused mid-bite.

"Maria is from Terrasini, Sicily," I said. "Grew up working in her family's restaurant."

"That explains why this place feels so authentic," she said, looking around again.

We focused on our food for a while. The hum of the dining room filled the space between us—low conversation, the clink of silverware, a chair scraping across the floor somewhere behind me.

She set her fork down for a second and reached for her wine.

"So when did they move?" I asked.

After a sip of wine, she said, "Right before my sophomore year of college. They'd always talked about living somewhere in Europe, so when the opportunity came up, they went for it."

"You didn't go with them?"

"No. I was already in school. It didn't make sense to transfer. So they packed up and moved to Scotland, and I stayed in Philadelphia."

"That's...a lot."

"It was," she admitted. "I think that was the first time I realized they were building a life that didn't automatically include me."

She paused, staring down at her plate for a second, dark hair falling forward. When she looked back up, something in her blue eyes had shifted.

"But I guess that's what's supposed to happen."

Another small shrug.

"I just always thought I'd be the one doing it first."

Before I could say anything, she pointed her fork at me.

"Okay, that's enough about me," she said. "I haven't learned anything about you."

"I'm an open book."

She chuckled. "I'm not so sure about that."

"Besides, for the wedding, it's more important that I know your facts," I said. "No one there's going to question whether you know me. They'll definitely notice if I don't know you, so I need to have my facts straight."

"Fair point." She picked up her fork again. "Okay. Go."

"Go what?"

"Tell me something I don't know."

I blew out a quiet breath. "There's not much to tell. I grew up here. Went to vo-tech for HVAC. Been working as a service tech ever since."

"That's it?" she asked, smiling.

"That's it."

She tilted her head slightly. "Did you ever want to leave?"

The question wasn't loaded. Just curious.

I considered it.

"Not really. I like it here," I said. "I like knowing where things are. Who people are. I like that if I drive down Main Street, I'll probably see someone I know."

"That sounds...steady."

"I guess it is."

I dragged a piece of bread through what was left of the sauce on my plate.

"Not everyone wants that," I added. "Some people want more."

She watched me for a second.

"Sounds like there's a story there."

I glanced up at her.

"Not one for tonight."

She held my gaze for a second, then nodded.

"Okay. I won't push." A small smile tugged at her mouth. "But just so you know...steady's not a bad thing."

I let out a small breath.

"Maybe," I said. "Guess it depends on who you ask."

CHAPTER FIFTEEN

"TWO WEEKS TODAY," Lauren said, lifting her Prosecco. "To the big day."

Nicole pressed a hand to her chest, her smile bright and a little breathless. "I can't believe it's finally almost here."

Glasses lifted around the table, the soft clink of crystal overlapping as we echoed Lauren's toast.

Kelly pressed her lips together and blinked quickly. "I can't believe my baby is getting married." She shook her head, half laughing. "How am I old enough to have two married daughters?"

Nicole's mom had always been warm, present, and emotional in a way that felt safe.

When my parents moved to Scotland, the Anderson house became my go-to place for holidays and weekends. Without hesitation, Kelly gave me my own space and treated me like a third daughter. She bought me cheddar Goldfish because she knew I was obsessed, gave me hugs when I needed them, and even held my hair back while I swore I was actively dying after my twenty-first birthday.

"Okay," Kelly said, lifting her glass again. "I promise no more getting emotional today."

Lauren laughed. "That's what you said after you cried at the alterations appointment."

"I did not cry."

"You absolutely did."

The table broke into easy laughter.

We'd spent the morning at the bridal shop for final dress fittings. Everything zipped. The hems fell perfectly. No further adjustments needed.

The sage bridesmaid dresses looked even better than I remembered—perfect for early May. We'd each taken ours with us, zipped into garment bags like precious cargo.

Nicole's gown fit perfectly, too.

When she stepped out of the dressing room, something tightened in my chest. Not from sadness. Just a quiet, *oh, wow* hit that happens when a moment lands.

Our food had arrived while we were still riding the high from the fittings, servers weaving in and out as we shifted glasses and made room without missing a beat.

Nicole snagged a mozzarella stick and leaned back in her chair. "Okay. Deep breaths. Two weeks. We are in the home stretch."

"Everything is handled," Lauren said. "The venue has the catering under control. The timeline's set. Photographer's confirmed."

"And the florist?" Sasha asked, arching a brow.

"That's the one thing still technically on my list," Nicole said. "I have to drop the book page flowers off by the end of the week." She looked at me. "Wait until you see them in person. The picture I sent you doesn't do them justice."

"They looked perfect," I said. "I already know exactly where I'm putting mine after the wedding."

"Of course you do," Kelly said with a chuckle. "It was definitely fate when you were assigned the same dorm room freshman year."

She wasn't wrong. If some housing algorithm hadn't paired Nicole Anderson with Jessica Harper, we might never have met.

"And the best part is that they're upcycled," Tara added. "Most of them would've ended up in a landfill otherwise."

Nicole pointed at her. "I knew you'd appreciate that part."

Tara had been trying to save the planet in small, determined ways for as long as I'd known her—and eventually she'd made a career out of it. She spent as much time outside as she could manage, claiming it was cheaper than therapy and just as effective.

"You'd actually love this place I hiked to last weekend," I said. "There's this waterfall about twenty minutes outside of Maplemoor. It's tucked behind a trail I didn't even know existed."

Tara's head lifted immediately. "A waterfall?"

"It's small, but quiet," I said. "And there's barely any signage. It feels untouched."

Nicole went very still beside me.

"Who showed you that?" she asked, trying to look innocent, but totally failing.

I took a sip of water. "Someone."

Kelly leaned forward. "Is it the same *someone* who's accompanying you to the wedding?"

"It is," I said. "Caleb claims it's his personal mission to show me Maplemoor beyond The Lochwell."

There was a collective pause.

"So..." Maya said carefully. "...what's happening with you two?"

"He's my plus-one for the wedding."

That seemed to satisfy everyone. At least no one pushed for more.

The rest of lunch passed in a blur of seating charts and overlapping voices.

An hour later, I was following Nicole up the stairs to her apartment.

She kicked off her shoes the second we stepped inside, sighing dramatically. "Wait until you see these."

"The flowers?" I asked, smiling.

"The flowers," she confirmed, already moving toward the dining table where a large white box sat waiting.

She lifted the lid like she was unveiling the crown jewels.

The book page roses were even better in person. Soft cream pages stamped with black print, the edges curled just enough to look intentional. If you didn't look closely, you'd never know they were made from stories that had once lived on someone's shelf.

"They're perfect," I said quietly.

Nicole blinked quickly. "I can't believe this is actually happening."

"I can."

She closed the lid gently and leaned back against the table instead of walking away.

"You seem...better."

"Better?"

"Calmer," she said. "Less like you're bracing for impact."

"That's flattering," I said with a chuckle.

"It's accurate."

I shrugged. "My mom said something the other day that kind of stuck."

Nicole waited.

"She said I wasn't embarrassed. I just—" I paused, looking for the words. "It felt like I'd lost some imaginary race."

"That's actually very you."

"I know." I shook my head. "Brett getting engaged so fast made it feel like he'd moved on better. Or faster. Like that meant something about me."

"And it doesn't," Nicole said immediately.

"No." I exhaled. "It just meant he moved on. I'm the one who decided that put me behind."

The word felt silly out loud. Behind. As if life came with a scoreboard.

"I don't think anyone was judging you," she added gently.

"I know that now." I looked down at the paper roses, smoothing one edge absently. "I think I was the one doing the judging."

Nicole stepped closer. "You didn't lose anything."

"No, but I almost did."

"What do you mean?"

"I think I convinced myself everyone looked at me differently," I shook my head, annoyed with myself. "I pulled away from my best friends. Not because you weren't there. Because I didn't want to see what I thought you were seeing."

Nicole stepped closer. "We were seeing you. That's it."

My throat tightened.

"I even caught myself at the bachelorette party thinking everyone was acting weird. Like there was some unspoken thing in the air."

Nicole tilted her head. "There wasn't."

"I think I was just projecting."

"Breakups suck," she said, reaching for one of the roses and smoothing the edge of a petal. "Especially when they take a friend group with them."

"Yeah." I took in a deep breath and let it out slowly. "Seeing him is still going to be weird."

"Of course it will," she agreed. "You two had a whole life together."

"And now we don't." I shrugged. "But it doesn't feel catastrophic anymore."

"That's progress."

I smiled faintly. "Yeah."

Nicole studied me for a second. "I'm glad you won't be alone."

"Alone?"

"At the wedding," she clarified. "I mean, obviously I'll be there. But I'm going to be slightly occupied."

"Just slightly."

Nicole pulled me into a warm, familiar hug.

"I'm glad you're back," she murmured.

I swallowed. "Me too."

"I should head back," I said as we pulled apart. "But I'll see you in two weeks."

"Two weeks," she echoed, her mouth curling into a sappy smile.

As I stepped outside into the late afternoon light, I took a deep breath of fresh, spring air.

For the first time, the wedding didn't feel like something I had to survive.

It felt like something I could enjoy.

caleb

THE GAME WAS ALREADY in progress when I pulled into the gravel lot of the Maplemoor Middle School baseball field. I grabbed my jacket from the back seat, killed the engine, then stepped out of the truck. It's the kind of early May afternoon that couldn't decide if it wanted to be spring or relapse into winter. The sun was out, but the air had a little bite to it.

I followed the sounds of cheers and shouts of encouragement to the field. The Ward cheering section wasn't hard to find. Not because we were obnoxious—though Luke was trying his best—but because we took up an entire stretch of the metal bleachers.

Luke and Haley were mid-row with Christian and Danny, our parents sat a few feet down, and my grandparents were at the far end.

Grandpa Ward had his hands folded on top of his cane, like he was holding court. Grandma sat beside him, her purse on her lap and a scarf pulled up around her neck, shoulders hunched against the chill. Both of them perched directly on the metal bench like it wasn't slowly freezing them into it.

Instead of continuing toward them, I turned back to the truck. I reached behind the back seat and pulled out the two folding camp chairs I keep there, just in case. The fabric was faded from summers, tailgates, and one memorable Fourth of July when Luke knocked over an entire cooler on them. But the frames were solid. Before shutting the door, I grabbed the blanket Murphy has claimed as his car bed. Gram wouldn't care about the fur.

I carried them back and, before greeting everyone, set them up. The moment she saw what I was doing, Grandma's face softened.

"Oh, Caleb," she called, like I'd done something extravagant instead of the obvious thing.

Grandpa narrowed his eyes. "We're fine."

"You're not fine, you're stubborn," I said, setting the chairs down in front of them. "And if you keep sitting there, your back and neck are going to be killing you tomorrow. Probably your hips too."

Luke, two rows down, cupped his hands around his mouth. "He's right, Gramps!"

Grandpa sniffed like he hadn't heard any of it, but he stood anyway, slow and careful, and lowered himself into one of the chairs like he'd been waiting for permission to be comfortable.

I held my hand out for Grandma and helped her off the bleachers and into the chair.

She sighed with relief and squeezed my forearm. "Thank you, sweetheart."

I nodded like it was nothing, because in our family, it was nothing. It was just what you did.

Mom leaned forward around Dad and looked at me. "You're late."

"I work until four o'clock. If the game starts at the same time, it stands to reason I'd be late." I dropped into the spot beside Dad and braced my boots against the bottom rung of the bleacher, glancing at the scoreboard. "What'd I miss?"

"Not much," Dad said. "The first inning was three up and three down for both sides."

Now we were in the top of the second and Teddy was at shortstop.

He stood with his knees bent, glove low, alert in that specific way a good shortstop is—ready to move.

The pitcher came set and delivered, and the batter swung late, sending a grounder skidding toward the hole between second and short. Teddy moved like he'd been launched. Two steps. Glove down. Clean scoop. He popped up and fired to first. The throw hit the first baseman's glove with a clean smack.

Our section erupted.

Luke stood up. "Let's go!"

Christian bounced in his seat. "*Did* you see that? Did *you* see that?"

Danny yelled, "TEDDY!" even though there was no chance Teddy could hear him over the rest of the crowd, the dugouts, and Luke's entire body vibrating with the need to be the loudest person on the planet.

Teddy didn't look toward the stands or showboat. He just jogged back into position and got ready for the next play.

I felt my mouth twitch. That was good.

Grandpa leaned forward in his chair, watching the field. "I remember you at shortstop," he said, like he'd decided it was time to pull a memory out of storage. "Same look. Like you thought you could will the ball to you."

I glanced at him and chuckled. "I think I did will it to me."

Grandpa's lips twitched, not quite a smile, but close. "You weren't half bad."

From anyone else, that would've sounded like nothing. From my grandfather, it was basically a standing ovation.

He kept watching Teddy for a minute, then added, quieter, "Feels like yesterday I was sitting here watching you and your siblings."

The way he said it made it sound like he could see the ghosts of old games layered over the present—kids in uniforms, my mom with a clipboard, Dad with a thermos, Luke running his mouth even at twelve.

I looked back out at the field.

"Yeah," I said. "Doesn't feel that long ago."

The inning moved on—pitcher missing the zone, catcher calling time, the opposing team's third-base coach gesturing dramatically like he was directing traffic in Manhattan.

I stayed mostly quiet, because there was something calming about being here. About this being normal. Familiar. The same chain-link fence. The same chalk lines. The same parents living and dying by fourteen-year-olds' batting averages.

And somewhere in the middle of that, the wedding next weekend edged into my thoughts.

Top of the list was a haircut.

"You need a haircut," Mom said.

I checked the time on my phone. "I'm surprised you waited this long to say that."

"If you did it the first time I told you, I wouldn't have had to tell you again," she said. "It looks shaggy."

Of course, Luke had to add fuel to the fire. "It is shaggy. You look like you're about to start a garage band."

"Watch the game," I said, nodding toward the field.

The next batter sent one high into the outfield. Our center fielder snagged it for the third out.

After that, the game moved the way middle school games do—bursts of chaos, stretches of waiting, and parents acting like it was October. By the time the teams lined up to shake hands, the sky had gone soft and gray-blue at the edges.

Parents started drifting toward the parking lot as dugouts emptied in waves. It took another minute before Teddy finally stepped out, bag slung over his shoulder.

Dad nudged my arm. "Last one out."

I didn't look at him. "Yeah."

"I wasn't that bad," I said.

Luke snorted. "You absolutely were."

Teddy reached us a few seconds later, dirt still clinging to his pants.

"Nice turn at second," Luke said.

"Thanks."

Grandpa reached into his jacket pocket. "Good game," he said, holding out his hand.

Teddy shook it without hesitation.

I didn't have to see it to know Grandpa pressed a folded bill into his palm. The same move he used to do to my siblings and me when we were kids.

Teddy didn't even look down. Just gave a small nod and tucked it straight into his back pocket.

Dad followed suit, but was much more conspicuous about it. He fished a five from his wallet and handed it over with a quick clap on Teddy's shoulder. "Keep your eye on that inside pitch."

I leaned closer to Luke and whispered, "We used to get a dollar."

Luke huffed. "Inflation."

"Seriously," I muttered. "Five bucks per game?"

"And if Haley's parents show up, it's basically a revenue stream."

"Nice."

Teddy tucked the money into his back pocket, trying not to smile and failing.

Grandpa was already looking back at the field like it was no big deal. Like he hadn't just passed along something he'd been doing for forty years.

For a second, I saw myself at fourteen, dust on my uniform, a crumpled dollar in my fist like it meant something bigger than it did. It always had.

I folded the camp chairs and slung them over my shoulder, following my family to the lot.

The boys were already arguing about where to eat.

"Pizza or burgers?" Haley asked Luke.

He shrugged. "Doesn't matter to me."

It absolutely did. He just didn't want the vote on record.

By the time we reached the trucks, pizza had won.

"You in?" Luke asked.

"Not tonight."

He looked offended on principle. "You're the worst."

"I've got a dog waiting on me," I said.

Mom gave me a look. "And a haircut to schedule."

"Dog first," I replied.

"I mean it," she said. "You can't go to a wedding looking like that."

"I'll handle it." I opened my truck door and tossed the chairs in the back. "Or maybe I'll try a man bun."

Mom stopped mid-step. "Caleb Michael Ward."

Luke barked a laugh. "Three names. You're in trouble."

Dad just shook his head.

"Don't worry, Mom. I've got it all under control."

I climbed into my truck while the rest piled into theirs.

As I pulled out of the lot, the field lights glowed in my rearview mirror.

Murphy would be pacing by the front window by now.

That beat arguing over pepperoni.

jess

I HEARD the music before I reached the bridge. It drifted across the river, distant enough that I couldn't make out the song—just the steady rhythm of it.

It grew louder with every step.

The Legends & Lore Festival was clearly underway.

Caleb stood at the far end of the bridge, hands in his pockets, looking exactly like someone who belonged there.

He straightened when he saw me. "Hey."

"Hey." I looked around. "Where's Murphy?"

"At home," he said as we joined the flow of people heading toward Main Street. "It gets pretty crowded."

"That makes sense."

We crossed with the rest of the town—teenagers in Maplemoor High hoodies, parents hauling wagons, older couples carrying folding chairs like they planned to stay all night. A little kid clutched a balloon shaped like a dragon. Someone balanced a tray of lemonade cups that looked one jostle away from disaster.

The closer we got, the thicker the air felt—music, laughter, the low hum of conversation stacking over itself.

And then we stepped into it.

"Oh, wow."

Courthouse Square looked like someone had taken every cozy small-town idea and turned the saturation up.

Strings of lights zigzagged between the trees, already glowing even though it wasn't dark yet. Booths circled the green in neat rows—local honey in glass jars, handmade soaps stacked in pastel pyramids, a historical society tent lined with old photographs and pamphlets about Maplemoor's founding. A chalkboard sign announced live music every hour. The smell of kettle corn drifted past in warm, sugary waves.

Maplemoor had clearly understood the assignment.

"It gets bigger every year," Caleb said, scanning the booths like he was doing inventory. He looked at me. "You want to take a lap first or dive straight in?"

"Lap," I said. "I want to see everything."

There wasn't really a direction to follow. People drifted wherever there was space, cutting between booths, stopping mid-path to talk to someone, weaving around strollers and folding chairs like it was a contact sport.

Caleb angled his body slightly in front of mine when a group of middle schoolers barreled past, saving me from being trampled. I'd never really understood the appeal of tall men — Brett and I had always been nearly eye to eye, and that had never bothered me. Standing next to Caleb, I was starting to get it.

By the time we'd circled the green, my senses felt pleasantly overloaded. Caleb nudged us a few steps onto the grass, just far enough from the main flow of traffic to breathe.

"So," he said, glancing down at me. "Anything catch your eye?"

I glanced back toward the row of booths. "The historical society tent."

"Yeah?"

"They're selling Maplemoor Moose merch." I paused. "I feel like if I live here, I should probably commit."

"Careful," he said. "That's how it starts."

I headed toward the edge of the green where the historical society tent was set up, ducking around a stroller and a couple arguing about funnel cake along the way.

"Hey, Caleb," the woman said as we stepped up to the booth.

"Hi, Marilyn," he replied easily. "This is Jess. She's new to Maplemoor."

"Well, hello, Jess," Marilyn said, her smile immediate and kind. "Welcome to Legends & Lore."

"Thanks! So far, it's living up to the hype."

"When did you move to town?" Marilyn asked.

"A few months ago," I said.

"And where'd you land?"

"The Lochwell."

Marilyn brightened. "Oh! Then you should come by sometime. The historical society is actually in The Lochwell. We've got even more Maplemoor Moose merch there."

"Wait, seriously? How did I not know that?"

My eyes drifted past the pamphlets and old photographs, then landed squarely on the Moose merch.

T-shirts in three colors. Zip-up hoodies. Enamel pins. A basket of plush Maplemoor Moose, each wearing its signature tartan scarf. I reached in and sifted through them, turning one over, then another.

I felt Caleb watching me. "You know they're identical."

"That's what they want you to think."

He shook his head, smiling, and I turned back to the basket, only half listening as Marilyn launched into a story about last year's fundraiser and a tent that had apparently betrayed them in spectacular fashion. Caleb made the appropriate sympathetic noises.

I finally found a moose whose tartan sat just right around its neck. I gave it a small nod, like we understood each other, and tucked it under my arm.

Then I turned to the sweatshirts.

They were stacked in neat piles—heather gray, deep forest green, and a soft oatmeal color that looked like it belonged beside a fireplace. Some were pullovers. Others were zip-ups.

I picked up one of the hoodies and held it against myself, glancing down at the stitched outline of the moose over the left side of the chest.

The fabric felt broken-in, soft and thick enough to be cozy.

I debated between the styles, then set the hoodie down and reached for the zip-up instead. I found a gray one in my size and draped it over my arm.

Marilyn finished her story and shifted her focus to the merchandise in my arms.

"Looks like someone likes the moose."

"How can you not?" I said, setting the zip-up on the table. Then I reached for a small stack of Moose stickers and added three to the pile.

Caleb lifted a brow.

"For my tumblers," I said.

Marilyn smiled and began folding the zip-up with careful efficiency. She tucked the plushie into a brown paper bag with twisted handles, stamped on the side with the Maplemoor Historical Society seal in dark green ink.

"First festival?" she asked as she handed me the bag.

"First Legends & Lore," I said.

"It won't be your last," she replied confidently.

"Definitely not."

Caleb pushed off the table. "Thanks, Marilyn."

"You're welcome," she said. "And welcome to Maple-moor," she added to me with a wink.

We said our goodbyes and stepped back into the current of people moving past the tent.

Once we were clear of the crowd clustered around the merchandise, Caleb glanced down at me.

"You hungry?" he asked.

"Starving."

We stepped away from the historical society tent and let the current of people carry us toward the food booths. The closer we got, the more the smells layered over each other—fried dough, kettle corn, grilled onions, and the mouthwatering scent of barbecue.

A hand-painted sign advertised pulled pork sandwiches and brisket. Next to it, another booth had a banner that read *Pierogis & Haluski* in looping red script. I didn't hesitate.

I made a beeline for the pierogi stand while he headed one booth over for barbecue.

My mouth watered as a teenage girl handed me a paper boat stacked with potato-and-cheddar pierogis, sautéed onions scattered over the top and a generous dollop of sour cream on the side.

Caleb joined me a minute later, balancing a paper tray loaded with a pulled pork sandwich, an aggressive amount of fries, and two pickles.

I eyed the fries. "You planning to share?"

"Unlikely."

We'd see about that.

We carried everything toward the folding tables set up near the grandstand.

The band onstage wasn't loud rock festival energy. It was something softer—an older guy in a blazer with a silver streak through his dark hair, backed by a trio with a standup bass and brushed drums. He crooned into the microphone like he'd been doing it for decades, voice smooth and low, covering old standards with the kind of confidence that didn't need to shout.

It felt less like a concert and more like background music for a town that already knew how to entertain itself.

We claimed one of the smaller round tables set off to the side of the grandstand.

"So," Caleb said as he picked up his giant sandwich. "How'd you end up here?"

I dipped a pierogi into sour cream and took a bite, buying myself a second.

"I came to the Fall Festival once with my parents when I was a teenager," I said.

He blinked. "I didn't realize you'd been here before."

"Just the one time, but I remember thinking it felt… easy. Like everyone knew each other, but not in a suffocating way."

He nodded slowly.

"When I decided to move," I continued, "Maplemoor kept popping into my head. I'd only been here for a few hours for a festival, but I loved the vibe. People were so welcoming. It felt like they actually wanted to talk to you."

"You picked a town based on its vibe?"

"When you phrase it like that, it sounds questionable," I said. "But yes."

He considered that for a second. "I don't think I've ever chosen anything based on vibe."

"How would you pick somewhere new?" I asked.

"I'm not sure." He shrugged. "I've never had to."

And there it was again. The difference between choosing a place and being woven into one. Before I could push it, a voice floated over the music.

"There you are."

I turned to find a woman with the same warm eyes as Caleb, though hers were sharper, more observant.

"Marilyn said you were at the Moose tent." She smiled as she sat across from me. "I'm Caleb's mom, Linda."

"Jess," I said.

"I'll make sure he gets a haircut if I have to do it myself," she added, like it was part of her introduction.

Caleb groaned. "Mom."

"You can't go to a wedding looking like you're starting a folk band."

I laughed before I could stop myself. But honestly, Caleb's hair looked perfectly fine to me.

Behind her, a woman with a dark, razor-sharp chin-length bob and the kind of confidence that didn't ask permission walked up, already reaching for an empty chair. Her hand was laced with another woman's—tall, elegant, calm.

Without hesitation, they pulled out two chairs and sat.

"Nora," Caleb muttered under his breath.

"You must be Jess," Nora said, offering a quick, assessing smile.

"This is my sister Nora and her girlfriend, Lucia," Caleb said.

Lucia gave me an easy grin. "Welcome to the family circus."

Nora snort-laughed. "Like yours is any calmer."

Lucia tilted her head toward me and whispered, "She's not wrong."

The band shifted into something livelier, brushed drums turning brighter. A couple started dancing near the stage. Someone cheered.

Linda launched into a story about the year a storm knocked out the power halfway through the festival, Nora interrupting to correct her version of events before she'd made it three sentences in. Lucia leaned toward me to whisper commentary like we were already on the same team.

I'd told Caleb I loved the vibe here.

Turns out, this was it.

caleb

AT SOME POINT between Mom sitting down and Nora stealing fries off my tray, the table stopped being Jess and me getting to know each other and turned into a full-family summit.

I'm not entirely sure how it happened.

One minute it was just us. The next, Luke and Haley had appeared, Emily and Jason weren't far behind, and Mom was announcing, "We're going to need a bigger table," like she was coordinating a military operation.

Five minutes later, we were relocating.

Luke's boys were nowhere in sight, which meant they were either at the gaming tent or about to reappear asking for more cash. Emily's kids, on the other hand, had already locked onto the table like it had gravitational pull.

Anna clutched a cloud of pink cotton candy with the kind of reckless confidence only a seven-year-old possesses. Sam hovered beside her, inhaling kettle corn by the handful.

I watched the cotton candy and did the math.

Anyone within arm's reach wasn't getting out

unscathed. That included Jess, who had just pulled on her new Maplemoor Moose sweatshirt like she trusted the world. But sticky-fingered kids can't be trusted.

When Anna shifted in her seat, the cotton candy flopped in her hand. Jess caught it before it brushed her sweatshirt and sent it back where it belonged.

Without missing a beat, she laughed at something Jason said, like the interruption had barely registered.

Mom had already covered the basics—where Jess grew up, what she did for work, how long she'd been in Maplemoor. We'd moved past polite questions and into the part of the night where embarrassing childhood stories made their inevitable appearance.

Jess was laughing. Not polite laughter. Not the tight kind people use when they're trying to survive a first meeting. It was a full-on, head tipped back, belly laugh. I was pretty sure I heard her snort once.

She didn't seem fazed by my family in the slightest.

Meanwhile, Mom was acting like this wasn't a one-off. Like I'd be bringing her around regularly.

Jess excused herself when Emily mentioned the restroom, Lucia following behind them.

"She's great," she said, low enough that Mom couldn't hear.

"We're just going to a wedding together," I said.

Nora's mouth twitched. "Sure."

I dragged a hand down my face. Arguing with her would only make it worse, so I let it go.

The women made their way back a few minutes later. Jess slid into her seat.

"What'd I miss?" she asked.

"Nothing that won't resurface at Thanksgiving," Nora said.

Mom circled back to the story she'd been telling before the restroom detour—something about me, a garden hose, and an ill-advised homemade slip-and-slide.

Conversations split and re-formed. Mom moved from embarrassing childhood anecdotes to asking Jess about the wedding next weekend. Emily chimed in with unsolicited packing advice. Nora argued with Luke about whether the band this year was better than last year's lineup.

Jess held her own in all of it.

She asked questions. She answered them. She laughed —still the real kind.

By the time the singer leaned into the mic and announced the final song, the square had thinned out. A few booths were dark now, vendors stacking crates under the string lights. The air had cooled enough that people were tugging sleeves over their hands.

Emily looked down at Anna, whose head had tipped against her shoulder.

"That's our cue," she said. "We don't want her getting a second wind."

Jason nodded, already gathering napkins and half-empty cups. "If that happens, we're done for."

Luke sighed and looked at Haley. "Guess we better go track down the boys before they try to sleep in the gaming tent."

Mom stood and pulled Jess into a quick hug.

"It was so nice to meet you," she said. "Have a great time next weekend."

"It was nice meeting you, too." Jess smiled. "And thank you. I think it's going to be fun."

Fun.

That was new.

I looked at Jess. "I'll walk you."

She shook her head. "You don't have to."

"You've met my mother," I said. "I absolutely do."

That got a laugh.

"Fair," she said.

We fell into step side by side, the noise of the square fading behind us as we moved farther down Main Street.

"My family can be a lot," I said after a minute.

Jess glanced over at me with a smile. "I really liked them."

"Yeah?"

"Families like yours are why I like it here."

I glanced back toward the square. Growing up, I'd taken all of it for granted—the noise, the showing up, the way no one ever had to ask twice. Hearing someone else say it out loud made me realize how much I still counted on it.

We were still on Main Street when I saw her.

Rachel.

She was near the curb outside the hardware store, phone in hand. She looked up at the sound of footsteps and paused when she saw me. And then her eyes shifted to Jess.

There was no changing direction without making it obvious. So we kept walking.

"Hey," she said.

"Hey."

"I saw your whole family over there," she added, nodding back toward the square. "Figured that's where you'd be."

"That's usually a safe bet," I said.

Her mouth twitched like she almost smiled.

"This is Jess," I said.

Rachel's gaze settled on her more deliberately this time. "Nice to meet you."

"You too," Jess said, smiling.

An uncomfortable beat passed, long enough to be noticeable.

"Well," Rachel said, shifting her weight. "Good to see you."

"You too."

She gave one last look—not at me, at Jess—and then went back to scrolling.

We started walking again. Jess didn't say anything for half a block.

Then, casually, she said, "Friend?"

I looked over at her. "No."

She held my gaze.

"She's my Brett."

Jess nodded once. "Got it."

Two words. No follow-up questions, no look of pity. Just acknowledgment and forward motion. I wasn't sure why that felt like exactly the right thing.

We crossed the bridge in quiet after that, the river dark beneath us.

The Lochwell came into view, lights glowing in the lobby windows.

At the entrance, she turned toward me.

"Thanks for walking me."

"Of course."

She hesitated a second. "So...Wednesday?"

"Yeah?"

"You're working here, right?"

"Yeah, I'm done at four."

"I could meet you at The Brewhouse before book club so we can finalize plans for Friday."

"Sounds good."

"Goodnight, Caleb."

"Night."

She stepped toward the doors, then stopped and looked back.

"Thanks for tonight. I had a really good time."

"Yeah," I said. "Me too."

She turned and disappeared inside.

I stood there another second. Maplemoor had always just been home—the place I knew, the people I knew, the life I'd built without thinking too hard about it. Tonight felt like the first time I'd actually seen it through someone else's eyes.

Tonight, it felt different.

WHEN I OPENED THE DOOR, I froze.

Then I blinked. Twice.

He got a haircut.

Not a trim. Not a polite clean-up.

A full, intentional, wedding-level haircut.

It changed his face.

The longer waves that used to fall over his collar were gone, replaced with something shorter on the sides, a little more structured on top. Styled. On purpose.

His jaw looked sharper, his cheekbones more defined. He wore khakis and a button-down in soft slate blue — the kind meant to be worn untucked. No tie, no jacket. Just crisp enough to say *I made an effort* without trying too hard. And his eyes, which had always read as hazel, looked almost green against the color.

"What?"

That single word made me realize I'd been staring.

"Nothing," I said automatically, moving back so he could come inside.

He stepped inside and looked at me, one brow raised.

"You got a haircut."

"I did." He rubbed the back of his neck. "Apparently I'm not allowed to attend weddings looking like I'm starting a folk band."

I laughed. "It looks good."

"Yeah?"

"Yeah."

He'd been firmly in cute territory before.

This was…something else.

I wasn't sure I'd packed for this version of him.

He looked down at my suitcase and the garment bag draped over it.

"Is this everything?"

"I think so." I looked around the living room, doing a mental inventory of what I'd packed. "Yes," I added, more confidently than I felt.

Caleb's mouth twitched. "That didn't sound convincing."

"It was," I said, grabbing my suitcase.

He stepped forward and took it from me. "I've got it."

"It's not that heavy."

"Again, you've met my mother," he said. "I'm not risking it."

I rolled my eyes. He grabbed the garment bag too, and I followed him out, locking the door behind us.

We headed down to his truck, the afternoon sun warming the pavement. I slid into the passenger seat while he loaded the bags into the back.

He climbed in a second later, started the engine, and eased us through The Lochwell complex toward Main Street. I watched in the side mirror until the building disappeared from view.

I shifted and rested my arm on the center console.

"Where's Murphy this weekend?"

"He's with my parents, so he'll be spoiled beyond reason."

"A weekend with the grandparents? He's living the dream."

"He'll gain ten pounds," he said. "My mom gives him whatever she's eating. Plus treats. Plus he gets whatever my dad sneaks him when she's not looking."

"He probably loves it."

"He does."

He merged onto the highway, and the town fell away behind us as we picked up speed. The sky stretched wide and blue, the sun high enough to make everything look sharper.

"So," I said once we were cruising. "Rachel."

The noise he made was a cross between a hum and a grunt.

"What's the story there?"

He didn't answer right away, then finally let out a slow breath.

"We were engaged."

I understood that kind of loss. Not the ring or the title, but the future you'd already started building in your head. The one that disappeared before you got to live it.

"What happened?"

"She decided getting married and settling down in Maplemoor wasn't for her."

"How long ago?"

"Almost five years."

That was long enough to build a new life.

And from what I'd seen so far, he had.

The highway hummed beneath us.

I stared out at the road and let the silence stretch.

"We dated sophomore year in high school until she graduated college. Then we got engaged," he continued.

"That's a long time."

"Yeah." His thumb tapped against the steering wheel. "That's just how things usually happen in my family. Most of them met their person in high school or college and…that was it. They got married. Stayed."

There wasn't bitterness in his voice. Just fact.

"Nora always liked to call herself the black sheep," he said. "She swore she was taking a different path, but she met Lucia during law school and that was it."

"So now you're the black sheep?"

"Apparently." He huffed out a quiet laugh. "And my mom won't rest until I'm settled. Which, to her, means married."

He glanced over at me, then back to the road.

"I just want you to know," he said carefully, "I didn't tell them anything other than I'm going to this wedding as your plus-one."

I blinked. "Okay."

"I know my mom came on strong. And Nora likes to… imply things. But I didn't misrepresent anything."

There was something steady in the way he said it. Not defensive. Not distancing. Just clear.

"I didn't think you did," I said.

He glanced over at me, searching my face like he needed to be sure.

Something in his expression eased before he looked back at the road.

"I get it," I said after a second. "The mom thing."

"Yeah?"

"My mom wasn't pushing marriage," I said. "And she

definitely thought I was too young to move in with Brett when I did."

He glanced at me again, quieter this time.

"She wanted me to travel. Do things. Not plan my whole life at twenty-two."

"And you didn't listen."

"Of course not," I said. "I was in love. I thought we were building something permanent."

"And now?" he asked.

I hesitated.

"Now I think she might've had a point."

The air between us shifted. Not heavy, just thoughtful.

"Does she ever say I told you so?" he asked.

"Never." I smiled. "She's better than that."

"That's dangerous."

"Why?"

"Means she knows she doesn't have to."

I laughed.

"So basically," I said, "we both thought we had it all figured out before our frontal lobes were fully developed."

He huffed out a quiet laugh. "That's one way to put it."

Traffic thickened as we got closer to the city. Signs for exits stacked closer together. Philly's skyline appeared in the distance, and soon we were surrounded by crosswalks, horns, and people moving like they had somewhere important to be.

Caleb leaned forward slightly, scanning street signs and comparing them to the GPS.

"The hotel's a few blocks up. Keep an eye out for the parking garage. It should be on the right."

I smiled and looked out the window.

The city felt bigger than I remembered. Louder. Faster. Less forgiving than Maplemoor.

When I'd asked Caleb to come with me, it felt practical. I needed a steady presence in a room I didn't want to stand in alone.

But somewhere between then and now, we'd become friends. Real ones. The kind who knew each other's almost-marriages and family pressures and the versions of ourselves we'd outgrown.

"You okay?" he asked.

"Yeah." I nodded. "Just recalibrating."

He pulled into a spot, shifted the truck into park, and gave me a look like he understood more than I'd said.

And just like that, we were here.

caleb

I'D BEEN to enough weddings to know how rehearsals went.

Someone told you where to stand. Someone else forgot. Everybody pretended they'd remember tomorrow.

So when I got to the courtyard and saw people already lined up near the front, I knew I'd timed it about right—late enough to miss most of the standing around, early enough to walk into dinner with Jess.

I stayed near the doorway, hands in my pockets, just taking it in.

And then I found Jess.

She was standing near the makeshift altar with the rest of the bridal party, turned slightly toward the woman I assumed was Nicole while someone near the front talked through the last part of the ceremony.

I'd seen Jess a lot of different ways over the past few weeks—jeans, leggings, one of those oversized sweatshirts she liked, hair pulled back, no makeup.

This wasn't that.

Her hair was down, falling over her shoulders, and she was wearing a dress that skimmed her curves in a way that was simple but impossible to ignore.

It took me a second to realize what else was different. The heels. They changed everything about the way she carried herself. I noticed more than I should have, then turned my attention back to the rehearsal before I got myself in trouble.

Someone near the front clapped lightly. "Okay, one more time from the entrance."

The women shifted to the back of the courtyard as the men lined up in the front.

Same as every other rehearsal I'd ever seen.

As they waited, Nicole leaned toward Jess and whispered something that made them both giggle. Then she bumped Jess's shoulder, still smiling. She looked like every bride I'd known—excited, a little overwhelmed, trying to hold onto the moment while everyone else told her where to go next.

I leaned back against the stone wall and waited for it to finish.

A couple of minutes later, the music cut off and the officiant said, "All right, I think that's it."

The tight focus everyone had been holding onto loosened all at once. Shoulders dropped. Voices started up in low, overlapping conversations. Someone laughed, the sound lighter now that there was nothing left to get right.

The bridal party stayed clustered near the front. Nicole turned in a slow circle like she was trying to take everything in at once. Jess stood beside her, listening, nodding, and smiling.

A woman in a black hotel blazer stepped out from the

doorway that led inside, pausing just long enough to catch Nicole's eye.

"Whenever you're ready," she said gently. "Dinner's set in the dining room."

Nicole nodded, then clapped her hands and eventually the murmur of conversation stopped. "Okay," she said. "I think they're ready for us."

The group shifted again, this time toward a door on the other side of the courtyard.

Jess looked around and finally spotted me. Something in her face softened, like a breath she hadn't realized she was holding finally let go.

She said something quick to the bridesmaid beside her, then stepped out of the slow stream of people heading inside and started toward me between the rows of white chairs. I started walking and met her in the middle.

"When did you get here?"

"A couple minutes ago."

"Did we look as chaotic as it felt?"

"You looked like every wedding rehearsal I've ever been at," I said with a chuckle. "But it'll all be fine tomorrow."

She gave me a once-over, her smile widening when her eyes came back up to mine.

"Nice suit."

"Thanks." I glanced down at it. "Nora buys stuff like this for Christmas or my birthday. Probably in hopes I'll find somewhere to wear it."

Her mouth curved a little more. "Looks like her plan worked."

"Guess so."

She glanced over her shoulder, then back at me.

"Ready for dinner?"

"Always."

We followed everyone inside.

By the time we sat down, the room had shifted from drinks and appetizers to something more organized. Jess settled at the big table with the rest of the bridal party. I took the chair beside her.

Plates appeared. Glasses clinked. Conversation picked back up like it had only paused for a breath.

"Okay," the bridesmaid on my left said, leaning in. "How long have you two known each other?"

Her name was either Sasha or Maya. I'd been introduced to both, but I wasn't confident which was which.

"A couple months," I said, steady. "We met through my sister."

"She vouched for him," Jess added.

A few more questions came our way after that. Jess answered some. I handled the rest.

Across the table, Brett was watching.

Not openly, but I noticed.

He wasn't what I'd expected.

I'd imagined someone more genuine. Instead, he was polished in a way that felt deliberate.

Earlier, during happy hour, I'd caught him rising slightly onto his toes while he talked, like he was trying to gain an inch he didn't have.

Maybe I imagined it.

Maybe I didn't.

To use Jess's word, I got a bad vibe.

By the time dinner wrapped, voices were louder and laughter came easier. People started standing. Someone mentioned fresh air. Jess and I followed the flow back outside.

Clusters formed under the string lights. Laughter carried easier without the echo of the dining room walls.

Jess got pulled into a conversation with Nicole near the fountain. I stayed back a step, not hovering, just close enough.

"Caleb."

I turned.

Nicole's mom, Kelly, approached with a glass of wine, her expression assessing but warm.

"I'm really glad Jess didn't come alone," she said. "Weddings are easier that way."

"I'm glad I could be here," I said.

Her eyes drifted across the courtyard toward the groomsmen.

Then she looked back at me.

"Some chapters are harder to revisit than others," she said.

"This one doesn't seem to be," I said.

"No," she agreed. "It doesn't."

Kelly studied me another second. Not unfriendly. Just measuring.

"You seem...grounded," she said finally. "I appreciate that."

"I try to be."

"That's good," she said, giving my arm a light squeeze before moving on.

Jess found me a minute later.

"What was that about?"

"I've been vetted," I said.

She groaned. "Oh, no."

"I passed."

She smiled. "Of course you did."

We timed our exit with Nicole's aunt, which felt strategic.

Jess had done the rounds—hugged Nicole again, confirmed the morning's hair and makeup plans, and when there was a natural lull, she tipped her head toward the lobby.

"Ready?"

"Yep."

After saying our final goodbyes, we headed into the hotel and stepped into the waiting elevator.

Jess leaned back against the wall, arms folded loosely, like she was giving herself a hug.

"You okay?" I asked.

"Yeah." She nodded. "That went better than expected."

"That's your official review?"

"Mm-hmm." She shrugged. "It was weird for like thirty seconds, but then it was fine."

She didn't look rattled or upset. If anything, she seemed...settled.

The doors opened on our floor.

As soon as we stepped into the room, she took off her shoes then sat on the edge of her bed and rubbed her feet.

"Those shoes look amazing, but I'd be lying if I said they're comfortable." She stuck her legs straight out and wiggled her toes before standing again. "Plus Brett hated if I was taller than him, so it's been a long time since I wore heels."

There was a lot I could've said about that, but I kept it to myself.

She grabbed her toiletry bag and disappeared into the bathroom, the door clicking shut behind her.

I loosened my tie, draped it over the chair, and toed off my shoes. The room felt quieter now—no low hum of conversation, no polite laughter. Just the faint rush of water starting behind the door and the steady hum of the air conditioner.

When she came back out in an oversized T-shirt and leggings, hair in a scrunchie, the polished version from earlier was gone and she was just Jess again.

"My turn," I said as I headed into the bathroom.

The light in there was too bright after the dim room. I leaned on the counter for a second before reaching for my toothbrush.

I brushed my teeth, staring at the mirror, replaying the night in pieces.

Jess had slipped right back into that group like she'd never left. The inside jokes. The easy touches. It was obvious they were tight.

And Nicole's family had clearly filled in a lot once Jess's parents moved to Scotland. Kelly treated her like she was one of her daughters.

She'd told me why she moved. I'd never stopped to think about who she left behind.

I shut off the light and went back into the room. It was dark now except for the clock on the nightstand.

She was on her side, facing the wall.

I eased into bed, careful not to make noise. I'd just settled under the covers when I heard her soft voice.

"Thanks," she said.

"For what?"

"Being here."

"I'm glad I could come."

She made a small sound—something like "okay"—and then her breathing evened out.

I lay there for a minute, staring at the ceiling.

She'd made my job easy tonight.

No panic. No spiral. No reading too much into every glance across the room.

Maybe the buildup had been worse than the actual moment. Maybe once she saw Brett—really saw him—the memory of him lost whatever weight it had been carrying.

If tonight was any indication, tomorrow would be fine.

THE CEREMONY WENT EXACTLY the way it was supposed to.

Nicole glowed. The vows were perfect. I fixed her train twice and cried once.

By the time dinner was halfway over, the bridal party table had settled into that loud, overlapping rhythm that only happens when everyone's comfortable. The DJ had something low playing in the background, but it was barely audible over the hum of conversation.

Tara leaned toward me. "Okay. Be honest. Are you surviving?"

"I'm thriving," I said, lifting my champagne.

She narrowed her eyes. "You look calm."

"I am calm."

"That's suspicious."

I laughed and let my eyes drift across the table.

Brett was leaning close to his girlfriend, her hand resting on his sleeve while she said something that made him smile.

I looked away before I could think too much about it.

Tara was already mid-story about her new job when Henry leaned past her to say something to Caleb.

"...I'm telling you, the one by the overlook is better than Hawk Ridge," Henry was saying. "Less crowded. Better payoff."

Jim nodded from Caleb's other side. "You mean the one with the waterfall?"

"Yeah."

"If you want a great hike with a waterfall," Caleb said, "you have to do the one just outside Maplemoor."

Henry leaned forward. "So that's what...a couple hours away?"

"About that."

"How difficult is it?" Jim asked.

"There are a few rocky spots and some inclines, but overall it's not difficult." Caleb looked at me. "What'd you think?"

Four sets of eyes swung my way.

"I thought I was going to die at the one incline, but other than that, it wasn't bad," I said honestly. "And the waterfall is definitely worth it."

Maya blinked. "You went hiking?"

"And you survived?" Jim asked with a chuckle.

"What can I say? Maplemoor has inspired me to get out and explore."

That led to talk of them visiting for a weekend.

I didn't hesitate to tell them how much I loved that idea.

After the cake was cut and the plates were cleared, it was time to dance.

The champagne had been flowing steadily all night, and by the time the DJ officially opened the floor, everyone was ready.

Nicole and Brian started things off, and then it just turned into a party. In between fast and slow songs, we did the electric slide, the cha-cha slide, and even the chicken dance. That last one made me laugh so hard my cheeks hurt. And Caleb stayed with me through all of it.

He didn't hover at the edge pretending to tolerate it. He committed. Clapped when he was supposed to clap. Turned when he was supposed to turn. Even attempted the little shuffle during the "Cha Cha Slide" like he'd practiced.

Emily had told me he could hold his own on a dance floor. She wasn't lying.

The DJ's voice cut through the music. "All right, let's slow things down a little."

Caleb looked at me, lifted one brow, and held out his hand.

I smiled and slid mine into it.

His hand settled at my waist as we found the rhythm without trying too hard. I had to tilt my chin up to look at him.

"Thank you again for coming."

"Of course," he said.

"I didn't realize how much I didn't want to do this alone."

His grip didn't tighten. He didn't tease.

"You're not," he said.

His hand was steady at my waist. Mine rested against his shoulder. We swayed in place more than anything else, neither of us pretending we were professionals.

"How'd you learn to dance so well?"

He shrugged slightly. "My mom taught me how to slow dance. She said every man should know how."

"Of course she did." I tipped my chin up at him. "And the fast dances?"

"Lots of family weddings," he said. "And no real fear of embarrassing myself."

"That's a skill."

"You learn it fast when you're the youngest of four."

"That explains a lot."

His answering smile was quick and easy.

Around us, the room shifted into that quieter wedding energy. Couples closer. Conversations softer. Laughter still there, just lower.

For the rest of the song, I didn't think about anything else. I just let myself enjoy the moment.

When it ended, the room surged back to life, and the beat changed to something louder, faster.

Caleb's hand slipped from my waist. I swayed slightly before I caught myself.

"You okay?" he asked.

"Yeah." I smiled. "I think I'm going to use the ladies' room."

"Want me to—"

"No. I'm good."

I meant it. Mostly.

The hallway outside the ballroom felt cooler, quieter. The shift in temperature hit me all at once. I pushed through the bathroom door and braced my hands on the counter for a second.

The champagne had officially caught up with me.

My cheeks were flushed, my head just a little too light.

I washed my hands longer than necessary and looked up at myself in the mirror. My mascara was still intact, my hair only slightly less polished than it had been an hour ago. I leaned closer, blinking once, twice.

"You're restricted to water for the rest of the night," I said to my reflection.

I took a breath, straightened my shoulders, and stepped back into the hallway.

The music hit me again as soon as I opened the ball-room doors. And automatically, I scanned the room.

Oh. There he is.

For half a second, everything inside me shifted back into an old pattern. A quiet recalibration. That used to be my anchor point.

Then his fiancée stepped into frame.

Her hands slid up his chest. She said something close to his ear that made him laugh. He bent toward her easily, naturally—like that was where he was supposed to be.

She kissed him. Not dramatic. Not performative. Just comfortable.

And that's when it hit.

Not jealousy.

Not even longing.

Just the sharp, sudden awareness that eleven years doesn't disappear just because you want it to.

My body remembered before my brain caught up.

It wasn't that I wanted him. It was that I used to be the one in that spot.

The champagne made it land harder.

Like someone had peeled something back I'd managed to keep covered all weekend.

I knew I should've looked away, but I didn't. Couldn't.

I stood there a beat too long, and suddenly the room felt too loud. Too warm. Too full of history.

I blinked, swallowed, and tried to re-center.

But the reflex had already happened. And once you see it, you can't unsee it.

"Jess."

I turned.

Caleb stood just close enough that I could feel him there without him touching me.

He just looked at me. His expression didn't change or sharpen.

But I could tell he knew.

"You want some air?" he asked quietly.

I nodded before I could pretend I didn't need it.

He reached for me and guided us toward the doors.

The music swallowed us for a second, then the cool night air hit my face.

And I finally exhaled.

caleb

WE STAYED out in the courtyard for a few minutes. Long enough for her to find her balance again.

The night air helped. Cool. Quiet. Separate from the bass thudding inside.

Jess didn't say anything, and I didn't push her to.

When the ballroom doors opened and a small group spilled outside laughing too loudly, she straightened a little.

"You want to head up?" I asked.

"Yeah."

"Is there anything inside that you need?"

She held up her right arm, showing me the tiny purse dangling from her wrist.

"No, I'm good."

We slipped in through the hotel entrance to avoid the reception crowd.

The lobby felt almost empty compared to the noise we'd left behind.

"Sorry," she said once we stepped into the elevator. "The champagne hit me all at once."

"You don't have to apologize."

She didn't argue with that. Just leaned back against the wall, like standing upright took more effort than she wanted to give.

The ride up was quiet. The kind of quiet that felt more tired than awkward.

When the doors opened on our floor, she straightened and headed down the hall. I fell in step beside her.

Inside the room, Jess kicked off her shoes near the foot of the bed, then sat down like her legs had decided they were finished for the night. A second later she tipped sideways and stretched out across the comforter, still in the dress, one arm draped over her middle.

"You want to change?" I asked.

She shook her head against the pillow. "Just...give me a minute."

"Okay."

In the bathroom, I took my time getting ready for bed. When I came back out, she was still in the same position, her eyes closed, her breathing steady.

I left the light on. The soft glow trailed behind me as I crossed to my bed and lay back, staring at the ceiling.

"Caleb?"

Her voice was soft. Not asleep after all.

"Yeah?"

She didn't speak again right away. Just lay there, like the words were harder than they should've been.

"I don't want to be alone."

"I'm right here."

"I know, but that's...kind of far."

Something in my chest tightened. I turned my head toward her bed. She was still on her side, facing away from me. The space between the two beds suddenly felt bigger than the entire ballroom downstairs.

"Would you..." She swallowed. "Would you come over here?"

"Are you sure?"

She nodded. "I just don't want to be alone."

There it was again. Not dramatic or clingy. Just honest.

I pushed the covers back and stood, the carpet rough under my feet as I crossed the narrow strip of space between the beds.

Jess had already shifted toward the far side of the bed, and I settled behind her, close enough to feel the warmth of her through the thin fabric of her dress, but not touching, giving her the space to change her mind if she wanted to.

She didn't. Instead, she shifted until her shoulders touched my chest.

Heat pressed along my ribs, sharp and sudden. *Not now. It's not the time.*

After a second, I let my hand rest lightly at her waist.

She let out a soft sigh.

"I thought I was okay," she said quietly.

I didn't answer. Just listened.

"Seeing Brett didn't hurt the way I expected." Her voice was steady, but thin around the edges. "I kept waiting for it to. Like maybe I was just in shock or something."

My hand stayed still at her waist, but my chest tightened anyway.

"I'm not in love with him," she went on. "I know I'm better off without him. Honestly...looking back, there were so many red flags I just didn't see. Or didn't want to see."

There was no bitterness in it. Just clarity. And something like grief for the version of herself who'd believed differently.

She was quiet for a few seconds, and I thought maybe she was done.

Then—

"But when I saw him just now..." she said slowly, like she was choosing each word before letting it out, "it was like my mind just...defaulted."

My hand flexed at her waist before I made it still again.

"Defaulted how?"

"Like we were supposed to be standing next to each other. My brain didn't even ask if that was still true."

She let out a soft, almost embarrassed breath.

"It was muscle memory. Not love. Not longing. Just habit and history. Like my body recognized a pattern."

That hit deep.

"And the champagne didn't help," she added. "It made everything a little softer. Like my guard dropped without me noticing."

Her back pressed more firmly into my chest, like she was anchoring herself.

"For a second, it was like my brain went, *oh, that's who you're supposed to be with.*"

She paused.

"And then it caught up."

I let out a breath I hadn't realized I was holding.

"And what did it say?" I asked.

"That I already tried that," she said. "And it didn't work."

I tightened my arm around her, just a fraction. Enough to say I'm here and you're not wrong for feeling that.

Because what she was describing wasn't love. It was inertia. And inertia can feel an awful lot like fate if you're not paying attention.

"I don't want to go backward," she murmured.

"You're not," I said quietly.

She was still for a moment.

"Thank you for coming with me."

There it was again. Not grand. Not sweeping. Just honest.

I rested my chin lightly against the back of her head.

"Anytime."

I LIKED THE "OFF" weeks as much as the book discussions.

On book nights, we dissected fictional men. On coffee klatch nights, we dissected our actual lives—promotions, breakups, tiny wins that didn't feel like much until someone else celebrated them with you.

Those were the nights you couldn't hide behind a paperback.

And tonight, everyone was looking at me.

I'd grabbed tea from Vee on my way in and set my Brewhouse tumbler down as I slid into my chair. Ilona's eyes flicked to it.

"New stickers?" she asked.

Two glossy stickers sat next to each other—one that said *From Castles to Coffee Shops* and another that read *Your Escape Awaits.*

"Oh," I said. "Yeah. I fell down a rabbit hole."

Emily leaned in. "Those are cute."

"After we read *My Foolish Heart* last month, I binge-read

the author's backlist. Then I checked out her Instagram and saw she has this Passport Club thing, so I joined."

"It's stickers?" Leeta asked.

I nodded. "Custom ones delivered every month." I took a sip of my tea. "And honestly, who doesn't love stickers?"

"Right?" Carli said.

"It made me weirdly happy when the envelope showed up," I said. "I'm already kind of looking forward to the next one."

Emily set her mug down. "Okay. Enough about stickers. Tell us about the wedding."

I wrapped my hands around my tumbler and glanced around the table.

"It wasn't as dramatic as I thought it would be," I said.

Maggie tilted her head. "Did you talk to him?"

"When I had to."

"Was it awkward?"

"Not really." I shrugged. "Honestly, it didn't feel like I thought it would. I kept bracing for some big emotional collapse over him." I paused. "That's not what it was."

"What did happen?" Emily asked gently.

I hesitated, choosing my words.

"I had a...moment," I said. "I'd had too much champagne, and for a second, I forgot we weren't us anymore." I shook my head. "It wasn't about wanting him back," I said. "It was more like being on autopilot."

"Were you okay?" Alexis asked.

"Not immediately," I admitted. "But I got there."

"And Caleb?" Emily asked, casual but not.

I looked at her carefully.

He hadn't told her.

If he had, she'd be looking at me differently. Softer. Or amused. Or something.

But she wasn't.

She was just curious.

"He noticed and got me outside before it spiraled," I said. "We ended up calling it a night."

I didn't add the rest.

Instead, I looked at Emily and said, "I'm glad you suggested bringing Caleb. It would have been much harder alone."

She nodded. "He's a good egg."

"Yeah," I said. "That's enough about me." I looked at Maggie. "How was Penn State?"

"Did you find an apartment?" Leeta added.

Maggie let out a breath that sounded half laugh, half disbelief. "We did, and I co-signed the lease."

"Oh, wow," Ilona said.

"I know," Maggie said, shaking her head. "It feels like yesterday I was dropping her off freshman year and crying the entire drive home."

"You did cry," Emily said gently.

"I absolutely did," Maggie replied. "And now she's finishing up freshman year. It's insane how fast it goes."

"Time is rude," Alexis said softly.

"It really is," Maggie said. "It's still an adjustment. It was just the two of us for so many years and now she doesn't need me in the same way."

The table went quiet for half a beat after that.

Not heavy. Just the kind of quiet that happens when something true lands.

"She still needs you," Alexis said gently. "Just… differently."

"I know. And that's good. That's the goal." Maggie smiled. "It doesn't make it easier."

We all nodded, collectively agreeing to the fact that

time keeps moving whether we're emotionally prepared for it or not.

The conversation shifted again after that.

Ilona announced she was training for a half marathon "for fun." None of us believed it. Leeta was finalizing graduation logistics and pretending she wasn't emotionally attached to every eighth grader. And Alexis was asking for tips on how to keep her two-year-old in his own bed.

I laughed in the right places. Asked follow-up questions. Listened.

But somewhere in the back of my mind, something was still turning over.

She doesn't need me the same way anymore.

Things shift. Not dramatically. Not all at once. Just gradually enough that you don't notice until you're standing in a different version of your life.

Eventually chairs scraped back and mugs emptied. We lingered the way we always did, nobody quite ready to be the first one to call it.

Outside, the air was cool but not cold. Early spring trying to decide what it wanted to be. By the time I let myself into my apartment, the energy from The Brewhouse had worn off.

I dropped my keys into the bowl by the door and kicked off my shoes, nudging them toward the wall with my toe. The place was quiet in that steady, familiar way that usually felt comforting.

Tonight it just felt...quiet.

I settled onto the couch, reaching for the remote. I opened Netflix and turned on *Gilmore Girls*, letting the familiar dialogue fill the room.

After a minute, I grabbed my phone and opened my calendar to check what I had going on tomorrow. A proposal to put the finishing touches on in the morning, a Zoom at noon about another project, and a two-hour block I'd optimistically labeled "admin."

I scrolled. Then scrolled back up like I'd missed something.

The last few weeks had been packed with wedding prep and getting-to-know-you sessions with Caleb.

Now Nicole is on her honeymoon, and Caleb is...I'm not sure.

It just felt strange. I'd gotten used to seeing his name pop up in my week, used to thinking, *I'll tell Caleb that later.*

I set my phone down and leaned back into the couch cushions, staring at the ceiling while the TV murmured in the background.

We didn't have a reason to get together anymore.

Except I kind of wanted to.

I liked spending time with Caleb. And I thought we'd become friends.

Would it be weird if we still hung out?

Before I could overthink it, I picked my phone back up and typed a message.

> Do you and Murphy want to go on a hike this weekend?

I hit send.

caleb

MURPHY LIFTED his head the second my phone buzzed, like he thought it might be about him.

I glanced down at the screen.

> Do you and Murphy want to go on a hike this weekend?

Actually...it sort of was.

I read it once. Then again, just to make sure.

Murphy's tail thumped once against the floor. Slow. Expectant. Like he already knew what I was going to say.

> We're free. Are you up for somewhere new?

> Sounds fun!

> How's Saturday at nine? We'll pick you up.

> Perfect! See you then.

I set my phone down.

"Looks like we're going hiking with Jess this weekend."

Murphy stood up immediately—ears forward, body already angled toward the door like we were leaving right now. His tail sped up, thumping against the floor.

"It says *weekend*," I said, scratching behind his ears. "Not 'in the next thirty seconds.'"

Murphy huffed.

I didn't know if that meant agreement or attitude.

Probably both.

I stood and shoved my phone in my pocket.

"Come on," I said. "Let's go play catch."

He ran ahead of me and waited at the door.

I grabbed the tennis ball off the patio table and lobbed it into the yard. Murphy took off after it and returned a second later, dropping it at my feet. I threw it again. And again. After a few more rounds, instead of coming back, he flopped down next to it.

"Done?" I asked.

He stretched out, tongue lolling, eyes half-closed.

Guess so.

I dropped into one of the patio chairs and dragged a hand through my hair.

The last few days had been quiet without Jess.

I hadn't realized how used to seeing her I'd gotten over the past few weeks.

It felt good to have plans with her again.

* * *

The ground was marshy in spots and Murphy had taken it as a personal challenge to run through each one.

By the time we reached the parking lot, his paws were caked in mud.

I opened the back door of the truck. Murphy moved like he was about to jump in.

"Hold it," I said, catching his collar before he could. "You're not getting in like that."

He looked offended.

I reached into the storage bin and grabbed the old towel I kept back there for exactly this reason.

"Sit."

He didn't.

"Murphy."

He sat, and I crouched down and grabbed one muddy paw, wiping it off as best I could.

"Do you have another towel?" Jess asked.

I glanced up. "Why?"

She pointed. "His whole side is streaked with mud."

"Yeah, there's one in the door pocket."

I shifted to Murphy's back paws, lifting one carefully and wiping along the pads. Out of the corner of my eye, I saw Jess lean into the truck. She straightened with the other towel and stepped in beside me.

Without hesitation, she went to work, brushing the mud off Murphy's side in slow, steady strokes.

Murphy leaned into her hand, practically melting against her leg, his tongue lolling like she'd just upgraded his entire experience.

"Traitor," I muttered.

She smiled, focused on a streak near his shoulder. "He's such a sweetheart."

"He ran through every puddle we passed."

"That's commitment," she said. "I respect it."

Murphy leaned harder into her.

"Good to know where his loyalty stands," I said.

She grinned. "He has excellent judgment."

"Yes, he does."

I watched them for a second. Her hair had slipped loose from whatever had been holding it back. There was a streak of dirt across her knuckles now, and she didn't seem to notice.

"I'm starving. Want to grab lunch?"

She gave Murphy one last swipe and straightened. "Yeah. I'd like that."

I took the towel from her and tossed both into the bed of the truck.

"There's a place just down the road with a dog-friendly patio."

"Sounds good."

Murphy hopped into the backseat while Jess climbed into the passenger seat, brushing her hands together before pulling the door shut.

I got behind the wheel and pulled out of the parking lot. Five minutes later, we were easing into a spot outside Willow Run Café.

The patio was already half full, a couple of dogs stretched out under tables like this was their regular weekend routine.

"Looks like his kind of crowd," I said.

Jess smiled as she glanced back, Murphy's tail thumping against the seat.

I stepped out and opened the back door, clipping Murphy's leash on before he could jump out.

Jess came around the truck, and we walked toward the patio together. A host grabbed a couple of menus and led us to a table near the railing.

"Bathroom?" Jess asked, holding up her hands.

"Through there, to the right," I said, gesturing toward the entrance.

She disappeared inside. I secured the leash to the chair leg and sat down.

The host set a bowl of water in front of Murphy and placed two menus on the table.

Jess came back out a minute later.

I stood. "My turn."

When I returned, she was scanning the menu, absently scratching Murphy's head.

She glanced up. "Everything looks good."

"The burgers are solid, but honestly, I've never had anything bad here."

The server came over, and we both ended up ordering burgers—hers with mushrooms and Swiss, mine with bacon and cheddar.

The patio buzzed around us, but it wasn't loud. Just forks against plates, low conversation, the occasional bark from a dog wanting attention.

"Do you hike that loop a lot?" she asked.

"Usually once a month or so," I said. "Depends on the weather. As you saw, it stays pretty wet. If we've had a lot of rain, I avoid it."

She glanced down toward Murphy. "He would *not* avoid it."

"No. He sees standing water and dives right in."

"He has fun."

"Yeah, he does."

"I admire his enthusiasm," she said with a smile.

Our drinks arrived, condensation already sliding down the glasses. She wrapped both hands around hers like she was grounding herself.

"So. Have you written any proposals for pain-in-the-ass buildings lately?"

She laughed and leaned back in her chair. "Actually, yeah. The one I'm working on now might qualify."

"Hopefully they'll get another company to install the HVAC."

"It's in Upstate New York, so I think you're safe."

"Whew!" I wiped my hand across my brow. "I didn't know your firm worked that far out."

"It was sold to a bigger company a few months ago," she said. "They're based in Rochester."

"How's that been?" I asked.

She shrugged. "So far it's been status quo. We had a Zoom with the regional manager and he said his business philosophy is 'if it ain't broke, don't fix it.'"

"That's good."

"I'm choosing to believe it is," she said, taking another sip of her drink.

I nodded once. "Well. If you need someone to evaluate structural integrity, I charge reasonable rates."

She smiled. "I'll keep that in mind."

The server returned and set our plates down in front of us, the fries practically spilling over the edge.

Jess looked at her burger for a second. "Yikes."

"That bad?" I asked.

"No. Just...big."

"I have faith in you."

She picked up the burger carefully, like she was assessing the situation, then took a bite.

I did the same.

For a minute or two, conversation gave way to eating. She kept having to adjust her grip as the mushrooms threatened to slide out every time she took a bite. I pretended not to notice when she leaned forward, shoulders curling slightly over the plate like she could shield the burger from gravity.

After a few more bites, she set it down and wiped her fingers on a napkin.

"So," she said, "are you still working on the jail conversion project?"

I shook my head. "No. I'm pretty much done there."

"That feels like a win."

"It is," I said. "I'm wrapping up another job now. After that, I'll probably be at The Lochwell for a while."

She glanced up. "Oh?"

"Yeah. They're replacing a few things. Nothing dramatic."

"Nothing muddy?"

"Hopefully not."

She made it through three-quarters of the burger and about half the fries before calling it.

Two napkins didn't stand a chance against the grease.

"I'm going to wash my hands," she said, sliding off the stool.

I watched her weave between the tables and head inside.

Today had been good.

Better than good, if I'm being honest.

I liked being around her. More than I had with anyone in a long time.

When I agreed to be her plus-one for Nicole's wedding, I hadn't expected to miss her when it was over.

I finished my iced tea in one long gulp.

I'd told Luke I'd stay open if someone came along who actually interested me.

Somewhere along the way, Jess had.

Murphy lifted his head when she sat back down, then settled again.

"Is he done for the day?" she asked, nodding toward him.

"He'll rally for our post-dinner walk."

She laughed softly.

Something in my chest tightened. Not uncomfortable, just certain.

I didn't give myself time to overthink it.

"Would you like to go to dinner Saturday night?"

She blinked.

"On a date," I added, in case that wasn't obvious.

Her expression shifted, surprise softening into something warmer.

"I'd like that."

NICOLE'S SUN-KISSED face filled the screen, all golden skin and post-honeymoon glow.

"Okay," she said, adjusting the phone and tucking a strand of hair behind her ear. "We're home. I have opinions. I have stories. I have approximately one thousand photos I will absolutely be sending you whether you want them or not."

I laughed and curled deeper into the corner of my couch. "I do want them. All of them. Especially the embarrassing ones."

"There are no embarrassing Brian ones," she said defensively. "He was glowing. We were glowing. It was disgusting."

"Good," I said, smiling. "You deserve disgusting."

Nicole grinned, then leaned closer to the camera. "Okay, so the water? Unreal. I don't know why we live anywhere that doesn't look like that all the time. And apparently I married a man who cannot paddleboard."

She launched into a story about Brian attempting to

stand, wobbling like a newborn deer before tipping sideways and taking out an unsuspecting couple who'd been floating peacefully nearby.

"I'm serious," Nicole said, still laughing. "It was ridiculous. I married ridiculous."

"You married a man who loves you enough to try paddleboarding on your honeymoon," I corrected.

"Yeah," she said with a sappy smile.

I rolled my eyes. "You're insufferable."

"I know."

"I'm so happy for you."

We talked about the food. The sunsets. The way time felt different when you didn't have anywhere to be.

When she finally paused for breath, she leaned back into her couch.

"Okay, your turn," she said. "How are things in Maplemoor?"

I tucked my legs under me and glanced around my apartment like it might provide talking points. "Good."

Nicole narrowed her eyes. "That's it?"

"There's not much to tell you that we haven't already talked about. Things don't change much here, so my days are pretty steady. But I like it. Sometimes I'm still surprised at how much it feels like home after just a few months."

"Even though you abandoned me in the big city," she said, "I'm really glad you landed somewhere that makes you happy."

"I didn't abandon you." I chuckled. "I just relocated."

"Same thing." She shrugged. "Anyway, Brian and the guys are dying to come to Maplemoor after talking to Caleb at the wedding."

"So my glowing endorsement meant nothing?"

"You made it sound cozy," she said. "Caleb made it sound like some kind of outdoor adventure catalog. So naturally, they're obsessed."

The group dynamic had always been predictable. We moved in packs. Chose the same restaurants. Took the same trips. For the past couple of months, I'd caught myself wondering if I'd stayed with Brett as long as I did because I didn't want to step outside of that dynamic.

"It really is great here," I said. "You should definitely come."

"We could do a whole weekend. You show us your favorite places. We hike. We go to that pub you mentioned. What's it called?"

"The Foundry."

"Yes. That one." She snapped her fingers. "We'll invade. It'll be great."

"That would be so fun," I said. "There's a loop Caleb and I did this weekend that ends at this overlook that's incredible."

Nicole leaned closer to the screen.

"Speaking of Caleb," she said. "I've been dying to talk to you about him."

"Why?" I asked.

"When you told me he was coming as your plus-one, you failed to mention how hot he is."

"You think?" I said lightly, like I hadn't noticed.

Of course I had. I wasn't blind. The haircut hadn't hurt. It had sharpened his features in a way that was hard not to notice.

Nicole rolled her eyes. "Don't play dumb."

"I was a little more concerned with your wedding than his jawline."

"Please," Nicole said with a snort. "I know you can multitask."

She tilted her head, studying me for a second.

"He seems like a really great guy. And it looked like you two...got along well."

I tried—and failed—to suppress the heat creeping up my neck.

"*Jess.*"

"Hmm?"

"You're blushing."

"I am not."

"You absolutely are." Nicole narrowed her eyes. "Is there something you want to share?"

I planned on telling her. I just wanted it to happen first. Turning one dinner into an event felt premature. And maybe I was a little afraid I'd jinx it.

"Caleb and I are going out Saturday night," I said. "On a date."

Nicole actually squealed. "Why did you not lead with that?"

"Okay, relax," I said, laughing.

"The fact that you and Caleb have a date is top-of-the-call material. I just gave you a ten-minute paddleboard recap, and you're sitting there casually dropping that like it's a footnote?"

I laughed, but my stomach flipped anyway. "Your honeymoon is objectively more interesting than my dating life."

"Not when it's your first *first date* in more than a decade."

"When you put it like that, it sounds terrifying."

"It's not terrifying," she said. "It's exciting."

I reached for my tumbler and took a drink, collecting my thoughts.

"You know we were hanging out a lot to get to know each other before the wedding?"

Nicole nodded.

"We got back, and I didn't see him for a few days," I said. After a second, I added, "I missed him."

There. It was out.

Nicole's expression softened immediately.

"Of course you did," she said gently. "Absence makes the heart grow fonder."

"I don't know if it's that dramatic."

"Mm-hmm."

"I just—" I exhaled, gesturing as I searched for the right words. "I don't want him thinking I invited him to the wedding because I had some kind of ulterior motive."

"I promise he's not even thinking about that. Don't overcomplicate it."

I huffed out a small laugh. "I'll try."

We said goodbye a few minutes later, stretching it out longer than necessary, like we always did.

When the screen finally went dark, my apartment felt still again.

I reached for the book on the coffee table and curled back into the corner of the couch.

Don't overcomplicate it.

"It's just dinner," I muttered as I opened the book.

My mind kept drifting. After reading the same sentence three times, I gave up.

With a quiet exhale, I set it aside and pushed to my feet, heading toward my bedroom. I was standing in my closet before I could overthink it.

My fingers slid hangers along the rod, brushing aside

blouses and dress pants until they reached the dresses I rarely wore.

I told myself that deciding what to wear on Tuesday for a Saturday date wasn't overcomplicating.

It was being prepared.

caleb

I'D RESEARCHED restaurants in three different towns before I decided on one.

Not because Maplemoor didn't have good places. It did. But I couldn't take Jess out anywhere within fifteen miles without running into someone I'd gone to high school with, fixed a furnace for, or, God forbid, one of my family members.

I didn't want interruptions or commentary.

Both of those had happened nearly every other time Jess and I spent time together, and I didn't want to split my attention tonight.

I parked outside The Lochwell and sat there for a second, hands resting on the steering wheel. I'd picked her up a dozen times by now—coffee, book club, the wedding—but this was different. This was a date.

I shut the truck off before I could talk myself into sitting there any longer and stepped out into the evening air. It was cool but not dark yet. The light had that soft edge to it, like the day wasn't quite ready to be over.

As I closed the door, I caught my reflection in the side mirror and took a second to check myself.

Dark jeans. White button-down, tucked in for once. Brown dress boots instead of the scuffed work ones. The Italian leather belt Nora bought me for my birthday a couple of years ago—the one I'd never really had a reason to wear.

Now I did.

I locked the truck and headed for the entrance. Inside, it smelled like coffee and cleaning supplies. I passed the elevator and took the stairs to the third floor.

Jess's apartment was second on the left. I knocked on the door, and when it opened, I forgot whatever I'd planned to say.

She was wearing a blue dress—knee-length, fitted at the waist, the fabric soft enough to move when she shifted her weight. Not bright. Not loud. Just...blue.

It took me a second to realize it was almost the same shade as her eyes.

Her hair was down, loose around her shoulders, and she had on the same heels she'd worn to the rehearsal dinner.

"Hi," she said, and there was a tiny edge to it. Not uncertainty exactly. More like she was bracing for my reaction.

I let out a slow breath. "Wow."

Her eyebrows lifted. "Wow good, or wow I should change?"

"Wow, like...wow," I said. "You look beautiful."

The corner of her mouth curved, but I could still see it—the flicker of nerves. She shifted her weight, smoothing her hands down the sides of her dress like she wasn't sure what to do with them.

"You look really nice too," she said quickly, like she was filling space.

"Thanks." I held her gaze for a second longer than usual. "You ready?"

She grabbed her clutch from the small entry table and locked the door behind her.

We headed downstairs together and stepped back outside. When we reached the truck, I opened the passenger door for her.

She smiled like I'd surprised her. "Oh."

"What?" I asked.

"Nothing. It's just...no one's done that for me in a while."

That didn't surprise me.

I held her gaze for a second, then gave a small nod and stepped back so she could get in.

Once she was inside, I closed the door gently and rounded the hood.

After settling behind the wheel, I started the truck.

"We've got a little bit of a drive." I glanced over at her. "There's a steak place out in Waypoint I've been wanting to try."

"That sounds nice."

"Less chance of running into half the town."

She smiled, but it felt tight.

I got it. I was wound a little tight myself. Maybe the nerves would settle once we got there.

The silence that followed wasn't uncomfortable exactly, but it wasn't us. Usually we filled space without trying. Banter. Side comments. Observations.

I kept my eyes on the road, waiting for our rhythm to click back into place.

We were a few miles out of town when she finally spoke.

"How was your day?"

"I installed a ceiling fan in my neighbor's living room," I said. "It should've been a twenty-minute job, but it took three hours."

"Why?"

"Because Mrs. Donnelly likes to talk, and I'm not good at cutting her off."

She laughed, and this time, it sounded more like her.

I glanced over at her. "How was yours?"

"Nothing exciting," she said. "Ran a couple errands, read a little bit."

The highway stretched out ahead of us, the sky fading toward evening. The quiet settled in again, softer this time.

By the time we crossed into Waypoint, the sky had dimmed and the streetlights were fully on. The sign for The Copper House came into view, warm light spilling from its windows.

I pulled into the parking lot and cut the engine.

For a second, neither of us moved. Then I stepped out of the truck. Jess had pushed her door open before I could get to it. I reached out and she took my hand, steadying herself as she stepped down from the truck.

"Thanks," she said.

Her fingers slipped from mine as soon as her heels hit the pavement. The sharp click of them echoed in the quiet as we walked toward the entrance.

Inside, it was dim and warm, copper fixtures catching the light above the bar. The dining room was full, the low hum of conversation rolling through the space.

When I gave our name, the hostess smiled and

motioned for us to follow her. She led us to a table for two in the back corner.

We barely had time to settle before a server appeared with water and menus.

"Can I start you with something to drink?" she asked.

"What cabs do you have?" Jess asked.

The server named a few, and Jess chose one without much hesitation.

"Bergmann Lager," I said when the server turned to me.

She promised to bring those right over and walked away, leaving us alone with our menus.

Jess studied hers like she'd be tested on it. I skimmed mine, even though I already knew I was getting prime rib.

The quiet stretched between us again, heavier than it had any right to be. We'd never had trouble filling space before. Now it felt like we were circling something we weren't saying. The menus gave us something to focus on besides each other.

A few minutes later, the server returned with our drinks, setting them down carefully before stepping back.

"Are we ready to order?" she asked.

"I'll have the prime rib," Jess said.

"And how would you like that prepared?"

"Medium rare."

The server confirmed her sides and salad dressing with a quick nod before turning to me.

"I'll have the same, except I'd like mine rare."

The server nodded and stepped away from the table, disappearing into the hum of the dining room.

"Great minds, right?" I said. She smiled, but it faded quickly. Her fingers curled around the stem of her glass, and she took a slow, steady drink. When she set it down, I said her name.

"Jess."

She hesitated, then looked up.

"This doesn't have to be different just because we're calling it a date."

The tension in her shoulders softened a little.

"That's very calm of you."

"I'm panicking internally," I admitted.

That did it.

She laughed—her real laugh this time, head tipping back slightly.

"There you are," I said quietly.

Her eyes warmed.

"Apparently I forgot how to act when it matters."

"It matters to me too," I said. "But we're the same people we were last week."

"When you put it like that, it sounds easy."

"It kind of is," I said. "I was nervous about tonight, too. Not because this is hard. Just because it's been a long time since I've been this interested in someone."

She didn't look away this time.

"Okay," she said softly.

And just like that, it felt like us again.

The rest of dinner came easier. The tension was gone and conversation flowed without effort. It felt like last week —only better.

By the time the check came, neither of us were trying so hard anymore.

Outside, the air had cooled. I opened her door again, and this time she smiled like she expected it.

The ride back was quiet, but not strained. Jess rested her arm on the console like she usually did. Somewhere between Waypoint and Maplemoor, I turned my hand over and waited. A second later, she slid hers into it. We stayed that way the rest of the drive.

I parked in front of The Lochwell and shut the engine off. For a second, neither of us moved. Then I got out and opened her door. Hand in hand, we slowly walked inside.

The elevator hummed its way up to the third floor, the space smaller than it had any right to feel. When the doors opened, we stepped into the quiet hallway.

She let go of my hand when we reached her door and turned toward me.

"Do you want to come in?" she asked.

I wasn't planning on staying long.

I was planning on kissing her.

"For a minute," I said.

She unlocked the door and stepped inside. I followed her in, closing it quietly behind us.

After setting her keys on the small table by the entry, she turned back toward me.

We stood there for a second, close enough that I could feel the warmth of her through the space between us.

My hands moved first.

Slowly, deliberately, I slid them to her waist. Not pulling her in. Just resting them there, giving her room to decide.

She looked up at me, and her hands came up to my chest. Light at first. Testing. Then firmer, her fingers curling into my shirt.

I looked down at her mouth and couldn't resist any longer.

Leaning down, I brushed my lips against hers once, twice, gently, asking a question. She answered by leaning into me.

The kiss deepened slowly, naturally. No rush. No

urgency. Just the steady realization that this had been building for a while now. My thumbs pressed lightly at her waist as she stepped closer, her hands sliding up into my hair.

Her lips were soft and warm, and when she groaned against my mouth, I felt the vibration in my chest. I pulled her closer and angled my head, deepening the kiss just enough to test the line between careful and wanting.

When my tongue brushed lightly at the seam of her lips, she opened for me without hesitation.

The taste of her wine lingered there, sweet and warm. I took my time, letting the kiss build instead of rushing it. Her fingers curled into my scalp, and that low sound I'd made earlier came back, deeper this time.

I stepped forward, guiding her back until her shoulders met the wall. Her breath caught as I followed, closing the last inch of space between us.

She fit against me like she belonged there.

The kiss shifted—deepening, growing heavier. Hungrier. Our tongues tangling as the wanting between us finally took up all the space.

My fingers tightened at her waist, flexing with the urge to either slide down and pull her tight against my growing erection or drift up and palm the soft curves pressing into my chest.

I wanted to touch her everywhere. But I wasn't about to ruin this by rushing it.

When I finally ended the kiss, I didn't go far. My hands stayed where they were, steady at her waist, like I wasn't ready to let go completely.

Her eyes stayed closed for a second longer, her breathing uneven against my mouth. Then, slowly, she opened them.

There was a softness there I hadn't seen before.

Not uncertainty. Not surprise. Just awareness.

Of me. Of this.

My gaze dropped down to her lips, glossy and slightly swollen from my kiss.

I brushed my thumb along the curve of her jaw, tipping her face up just enough.

And then I kissed her again.

Not hungry this time. Not searching. Just slow. Intentional.

When I finally pulled back, I rested my forehead against hers for a brief second, breathing her in.

I wasn't staying long.

But I wasn't leaving just yet.

CHAPTER TWENTY-SEVEN

THE RIVER MOVED SLOWLY beside me, late light catching along the surface as I walked the trail behind The Lochwell.

I kept my eyes on the current as the path curved along the bend, the soft rush of water over stone filling the quiet.

It didn't help.

My mind kept drifting back to this afternoon—to Caleb sitting at my kitchen counter in his uniform, sleeves rolled up, thanking me for lunch like I'd done something extraordinary, instead of opening a jar of sauce and boiling some pasta.

He'd eaten like it was the best thing he'd had all week. But it was the way he'd looked at me across the counter that stuck.

Something had shifted after our date Saturday night.

Once we'd gotten past that first awkward stretch, everything between us had felt easy again. Comfortable. Like we'd slipped back into something that had been waiting for us all along.

Only now there was more to it.

Something deeper.

Hotter.

Every time his eyes found mine now, there was a pause. A beat that hadn't been there before. The kind that made my skin tingle.

And when he kissed me, it felt deliberate.

Not flashy or performative. Just there, present in the moment. He wasn't distracted or impatient. And it wasn't simply a step toward something else.

I'd always liked kissing.

The slow kind, where hands wandered, mouths explored, and I lost track of time.

But in my experience, it usually felt like something to move through on the way to the main event. And I'd never really questioned that.

Until Caleb.

Because with him, it didn't feel like something to get through.

When he pulled me in, kissing me was all he was doing. No testing how far he could go. No rushing.

He just stayed there.

Slowly. Like he enjoyed it for what it was.

I reached the bend in the trail and slowed, watching the water move past the rocks.

A breeze skimmed across the surface, lifting my hair off my shoulders. I stood there for a moment before turning back.

It was funny how this thing with Caleb had snuck up on me.

There hadn't been fireworks or a dramatic first glance across a crowded room. We'd been acquaintances. Then friends. Now he was the first thing I thought about in the morning. And apparently the only thing I could think about while standing next to a perfectly peaceful river.

My phone vibrated against my hip. I pulled it out of my pocket and checked the notification.

Book club.

Right.

I turned back toward The Lochwell, the gravel crunching under my sneakers as the lights of The Brewhouse came into view.

As I opened the door, the bell chimed softly overhead and the familiar scent of coffee wrapped around me.

Vee glanced up from the espresso machine. "Hey, Jess."

"Hi," I said as I stepped up to the counter.

"The usual?"

"Yeah."

"You got it."

The place had an early-evening hum—not crowded, but not quiet either. Familiar voices layered over the low whir of the grinder, the soft thud of someone setting down a cup. I looked over the sweet treats in the glass display case. Vee had gone all in tonight—neat rows of her homemade pop tarts lined up on a wooden board, the glaze catching the light. Strawberry. Brown sugar. Blueberry. Cinnamon.

Caleb had mentioned once that the cinnamon ones were his favorite.

I made a mental note to grab a few before I left. And while I was at it, I'd probably take an apple fritter or two for myself. They were *my* favorite.

Vee slid the steaming mug of Book Club Blend toward me.

"Here you go."

"Thank you."

I paid, picked up the mug, and headed toward the back corner.

The ladies looked up as I approached.

A few overlapping hellos followed—Maggie's hello, Emily's quick smile, Alexis lifting her hand in greeting, Leeta's soft "hey." It blended together the way it always did.

I slid into my usual chair. We didn't technically have assigned seats, but somehow we always ended up in the same places.

Maggie's gaze lingered.

Not obvious. Not dramatic. Just...attentive.

She tilted her head slightly. "Did you change something?"

My hand stilled on my coffee cup. "What?"

"I don't know," she said slowly, studying me in that quiet way she had. "Something looks different."

Emily glanced at me, then back at Maggie.

"I was thinking that too," she said. Not accusing. Just matter-of-fact.

Heat crept up my neck. "I didn't change anything."

A small pause followed as they all looked at me.

I suddenly felt very aware of my face, specifically my lips. They felt swollen, but I knew they looked normal. I'd checked in the mirror before leaving my apartment.

The bell over the door chimed again.

"Sorry, sorry," Ilona called as she walked in, Tiff right behind her. "I got stuck behind a tractor on Main Street."

The room shifted instantly.

Chairs scraped. Maggie glanced toward the door. Emily leaned back.

And just like that, the attention wasn't on me anymore.

I took a slow sip of coffee and pretended my heart wasn't still beating a little too fast.

Once everyone arrived, Maggie kicked off the book discussion. Carli snuck in late and joined right in.

There was debate about whether the hero was afraid or simply careful. I listened and nodded in the right places, but wasn't focused enough to join in.

Emily's attention shifted suddenly.

She leaned back in her chair and squinted toward the counter.

"Caleb!" she called.

That caught my attention.

I kept my eyes on the page for a second longer than necessary.

Then I looked up.

He was already walking toward us, tucking his wallet into his back pocket. He was still in his uniform, sleeves rolled up, hair slightly mussed in that end-of-day way.

I had never really understood the appeal of forearms before.

Apparently, that had been a mistake.

"Long day?" Emily asked.

"Yeah." His eyes flicked to mine. "I'm just grabbing dinner."

Emily nodded as he looked back at her. "Jason dropped the Nesco roaster on your porch."

Caleb blinked. "Why?"

"For Anna's party Saturday. You're making wings, right?"

"Right."

She looked around the table. "He makes the best wings."

"What's your secret?" Leeta asked.

He smirked. "I use our mom's recipe. Emily likes mine better because she doesn't have to make them."

"That's not true," she said. "Yours do taste better. Everyone says so."

Caleb shifted his weight, one hand sliding into his pocket.

And then he looked at me. Not the quick glance from before. This time he held it long enough that I felt it.

Emily went still.

Her eyes shifted from him to me. Once. Then again.

The corners of her mouth lifted.

"Oh."

Caleb frowned slightly. "What?"

Emily didn't answer right away. She just looked at me, then back at him.

Maggie's gaze shifted too. Slower. More deliberate.

Tiff leaned back in her chair. "What?" she asked.

Emily sat back and folded her arms. "Would you two like to share with the class?"

I looked at Caleb.

He was already looking at me, his brow raised.

We hadn't talked about this. Not about what to call it. Not about telling anyone.

It wasn't a secret. We just...hadn't said it out loud to anyone.

Now the room was waiting.

I pressed my lips together, then caught the edge of my bottom lip between my teeth before I could stop myself.

A smile slipped through anyway.

"Yeah," Caleb said, his gaze still on mine. "Jess and I are dating."

A beat of silence followed.

Then Tiff clapped once. "Finally."

The rest of the table echoed the sentiment with easy approval.

Once they settled, Alexis looked at me with quiet amusement. "And you said the fake dating trope didn't make sense."

She wasn't wrong.

Emily glanced at Caleb instead.

"Jess is coming Saturday, right?"

Her eyes shifted to me.

"I..." I looked at Caleb, unsure what to say.

He held my gaze.

"If you're not busy," he said. "But be warned, my whole crazy family will be there."

Emily rolled her eyes. "We're not *that* crazy."

I smiled before I could stop myself.

"I'm not busy."

Emily nodded once, satisfied. "Good. That's settled."

Caleb lingered for another second before nodding toward the counter. "I should grab my food." He looked at me again—brief this time, but not subtle. "I'll talk to you later?"

"Yeah," I said, trying not to smile too much.

He walked back toward the counter, totally relaxed, like nothing monumental had just happened.

But when he glanced at me again, it wasn't subtle.

And neither was the way I smiled back.

caleb

JESS SAID she didn't need me to pick her up, that she'd walk instead. I still ended up at the bridge ten minutes early. Meeting her halfway seemed like a fair compromise.

The river moved beneath the bridge, bright in the sun. I leaned against the railing, hands in my pockets, and waited. A few minutes later, Jess appeared on the other side of the bridge.

She'd pulled her hair back loosely and a bright yellow sundress shifted around her knees as she walked.

She slowed when she saw me and smiled.

I pushed off the railing and met her in the middle.

"Surprise," I said.

It wasn't dramatic. Just matter-of-fact.

She shook her head, but her smile was firmly in place. "I'm surprised you didn't just show up at my door."

"I considered it."

"I'm sure you did."

"But this felt more reasonable," I said.

She stepped a little closer, sunlight catching in her hair. "You didn't have to."

"I know."

A quiet second passed between us.

"For what it's worth," she said, softer now, "I'm glad you're here."

There wasn't an ounce of annoyance in her voice.

She looked glad.

"You ready?"

She glanced past me toward town. "As I'll ever be."

I held her gaze for a second, then reached for her hand and laced our fingers together.

"Come on."

We stepped off the bridge and started toward Emily's house.

After a few steps, she glanced up at me. "Anything I should know before we get there?"

I huffed a quiet laugh. "It's gonna be loud."

"That's not helpful."

"I think you'll like them," I added. "But they can be...a lot."

She'd told me it had mostly been her and her parents growing up. Quiet dinners. Holidays where you could hear yourself think.

My family didn't really do quiet.

She bumped her shoulder lightly against mine.

"I can handle loud."

We turned onto Emily's street. As we neared her house, we could hear them.

Music. Someone arguing about the grill. A kid shrieking for who knows what reason.

Jess slowed slightly, taking it in.

"You weren't kidding," she said.

"I never kid about noise levels."

She laughed, and the sound did something steady in my chest.

"Ready?"

"I am."

"Okay," I said quietly. "Here we go."

I leaned in and kissed her. Not rushed. Not dramatic. Just enough that she felt it.

And then—

"Uncle Caleb!"

I straightened and saw Anna tearing across the yard, ponytail flying behind her, a pink rhinestone princess crown bobbing on her head. I barely had time to brace before she launched herself at me. I scooped her up, spinning once before setting her down.

"Happy birthday," I said.

"Mom said I can have two pieces of cake," she whispered like it was classified information.

"As you should," I said. "Do you remember Jess?"

She nodded.

"From the festival."

"Happy birthday," Jess said. "I like your crown."

"Thanks. Aunt Nora gave it to me."

Someone shouted her name, and she was gone.

Jess watched her sprint back toward the yard, crown bouncing.

I looked at Jess and smiled. "That's just an appetizer."

We walked up the driveway toward the backyard. The closer we got, the louder the music and laughter became.

Jess glanced at me. "Sounds like this is the place to be."

We rounded the back corner of the house.

The yard was in full motion.

Jason stood at the grill like he was defending it from a hostile takeover. Smoke drifted sideways in the breeze.

Folding tables lined the patio, already cluttered with wrapping paper and half-opened presents. My grandparents sat in lawn chairs like they were front row at a show. Kids ran between the yard and the neighbor's driveway like they had diplomatic immunity.

Jess slowed for half a second.

Not overwhelmed.

Just taking inventory.

"I don't think I know this many people," she said.

Before I could comment, Mom saw us.

Her whole face lit up.

"Caleb! Jess!" she called.

A few heads turned our way.

Mom crossed the yard, wiping her hands on a dish towel.

"I'm so glad you're here," she said, pulling Jess into a hug.

Jess laughed softly, a little surprised but not stiff, and hugged her back.

"I'm happy to be here," she said.

Mom stepped back, hands still on Jess's shoulders like she needed to make sure she was real. "You look beautiful. I love that color."

"Thank you," Jess said, glancing down at the dress like she hadn't thought much about it until just now.

Mom glanced over her shoulder. "Jim."

Dad was already heading our way.

He clapped a hand on my shoulder before looking at Jess.

"I've heard a lot about you," he said, smiling.

Jess didn't miss a beat. "I hope that's a good thing."

He laughed. "It is."

Mom looped her arm lightly through Jess's. "Come on.

You need to meet the grandparents before they start accusing me of keeping you hidden."

Jess glanced back at me for half a second.

I nodded and fell in step beside them toward the cluster of lawn chairs near the patio.

Introductions were made. Hands were shaken. A few polite questions about work.

Jess answered easily, smiling when Grandpa cracked a joke I'd heard a hundred times before.

After that, I introduced her to the uncles and aunts, most of my cousins, and a couple of neighbors who basically counted as family. She moved through it all like she'd been doing it her whole life. Smiled. Asked questions. Remembered names.

At some point, Mom pressed a plate into her hands. She tried a little bit of everything, then went back for more.

We ended up at a table near the edge of the patio, watching the kids tear across both yards like they had unlimited battery life. Every so often, a foam football sailed into view from somewhere behind the crowd, and I had no idea who was throwing it.

Jess tracked it all with quiet focus, like she was cataloging the chaos.

"Uncle Caleb!" Danny jogged over with a basketball tucked under his arm. "You playing?"

Apparently he hadn't gotten the memo that I had a date today.

I looked toward the driveways. The hoops were already angled toward each other, the space between the houses turning into an unofficial court. A couple of the older kids were circling. Someone had moved the cars out of the way.

I started to shake my head. Normally I'm a firm yes. Just not today. Not with Jess meeting everyone for the first time.

Jess's fingers wrapped lightly around my forearm.

"Go ahead," she said.

Mom smiled. "We've got her."

I looked at Jess. "You sure?"

"Positive."

"Okay."

I let Danny drag me toward the driveway.

By the time we called it, I was sweaty and winded. Luke had already bowed out after claiming a pulled hamstring that absolutely did not exist. Jason had been "just officiating," which mostly meant calling a foul anytime someone got near him.

Jess was standing near the patio with Mom, Nora, and Lucia. When I made my way back to her, she handed me a bottle of water like she'd been waiting.

"Have fun?" she asked.

"Always."

After a while, the party shifted into that familiar wind-down phase, and I figured it was a good time to head out.

I glanced at Jess. "I need to let Murphy out. Want to come along?"

Her whole face lit up. "Absolutely."

We made the rounds and said goodbye—quick hugs from Mom, Dad's hand firm on my shoulder, Grandma telling Jess she expected to see her again soon.

Then we slipped down the driveway and back toward the street, the noise fading behind us with each step until it was just the two of us and the sound of our shoes on the pavement. Her hand stayed in mine, warm and steady.

Two blocks later, I opened my front door and held it open for her.

Murphy was already there, nails skidding across the hardwood before I'd even closed it.

"Hey, buddy—"

He gave me a quick sniff, then launched himself at Jess.

She laughed as he wiggled against her, tail thumping against the wall.

"I know," she said, dropping to her knees. "I missed you too."

I let him soak up the attention for a minute. He deserved it.

"All right," I said finally. "Let's go outside."

Murphy bolted past me toward the back door. When I opened it, he shot into the yard, handled business at record speed, then came tearing back like we'd abandoned him for years instead of hours.

Jess and I followed him out and stood on the deck, watching him sprint in wide, unnecessary circles, clearly showing off for her. She picked up the tennis ball and tossed it once. Murphy chased it like his reputation depended on it.

We took turns throwing it a few more times, his sprints getting shorter each round, the dramatic flair fading.

Finally he slowed to a jog, tongue lolling, sides heaving.

"All right," I said. "You're done."

Once inside, he drank like he'd run a marathon, then collapsed in the living room with a satisfied thud.

I grabbed Jess and me each a lager and joined her on the couch. She'd kicked off her sandals and curled into the corner, and I sat next to her.

"So what'd you think of the party?"

"It was fun." She smiled. "Everyone was nice, the food was amazing, and your mom told me how you probably could have played in the NBA if you'd wanted to."

I chuckled. "I was Maplemoor good, not NBA good."

She tilted her head. "Still."

"It was fun," I said. "But it was never going to be more than that."

I took a slow drink from my bottle, the cold bite of it grounding.

I leaned forward to set it on the coffee table, and when I sat back, I shifted a little closer to Jess.

My knee brushed hers. She didn't move away. In fact, I think she moved closer.

Jess looked at me like she was still turning over the afternoon in her head.

"You fit," I said before I could stop myself.

"With your family?"

"Yes." I held her gaze. "And with me."

She went still. Not frozen. Just searching.

Her eyes moved over my face like she was searching for something.

Her hand tightened in my shirt.

"You mean that?" she asked.

"Yeah."

A beat passed.

Then she leaned forward and set her beer bottle down next to mine on the coffee table.

When she sat back, her thigh pressed against mine. Her hand slid up my chest and stayed there, warm and steady over my heartbeat.

"You have no idea..."

I wrapped my hands around her waist and pulled her in, pressing my mouth to hers. Not careful. Not tentative. Hungry.

She kissed me back the same way, as her fingers fisted in my shirt. I pulled her over until her legs straddled mine. My hand slid into her hair, tipping her head back so I could deepen it.

She made a soft sound against my mouth and dug her fingers into my scalp.

The kiss turned messy in the best way. Long, deep, tasting.

When I pulled back for air, I barely moved. My mouth brushed hers with every breath.

Her lips were swollen. Her eyes darker.

"Jess," I said, already pulling her back to me.

She just kissed me again.

CHAPTER TWENTY-NINE

THE SECOND OUR mouths touched again, everything else disappeared. The room, the party we'd just left, the sound of Murphy snoring on the floor—gone.

His hands tightened at my waist, and he shifted, rolling us so my back hit the cushions, and my head rested against the arm of the couch. A startled laugh caught in my throat, but he swallowed it with another kiss.

My sundress twisted high around my thighs, the smooth fabric of his shorts brushing against my bare skin as he pressed closer. His chest settled against mine, one leg nudging my knees wider, hands braced on either side of my shoulders as his mouth moved from my lips to my jaw, then lower—to the soft spot just beneath my ear.

A raw sound slipped from my throat.

He shifted again, closer, and I felt him—hard and unmistakable—through the thin layers of fabric between us.

I slid my right leg around his waist, pulling him closer.

He groaned, low and rough.

"Jess," he breathed against my skin.

The way he said my name made my stomach tighten.

His mouth found mine again, hungrier this time. His tongue moved against mine, slow and deliberate, his hips keeping the same steady rhythm.

I shoved my hands under his T-shirt, fingers curling into the warm skin of his back, pulling him tighter against me.

Caleb pressed forward, and I arched up to meet him.

The couch creaked faintly under us.

I should have felt overwhelmed by the size of him, how completely he covered me. Instead, I wanted him closer.

A bang sounded somewhere to my left, but it felt far away.

His mouth stilled against mine. He lifted his head slowly, breathing hard.

I blinked up at him, breathless.

"This is not the most ergonomic place," he muttered, voice rough.

"Are you okay?"

"Yeah. I just banged my leg on the coffee table." He blew out a breath. "We should move."

"Move," I echoed, nodding once.

His eyes darkened, then he reached down and guided my other leg around his waist, pulling me flush against him before sliding his hands beneath my thighs.

"Hold on," he murmured.

He stood, and I gasped as the world tilted. I tightened my legs around him, locking my arms around his neck.

I buried my face against him, kissing the warm skin just below his ear as he carried me. His chest rose against mine with every breath, his hands firm beneath my thighs, and with every steady step he pressed us closer.

He made it up the stairs without breaking stride,

nudging the bedroom door open with his foot before carrying me inside. I loosened my legs and slid down his body, hands still gripping his shoulders until my feet met the floor.

The bed looked enormous, made up with the same quiet neatness that felt so completely Caleb. A framed photo of Caleb and Murphy sat on the nightstand beside a lamp, its warm light softening the room.

The quiet click of the door closing made me turn back to him, and the look in his eyes stole the rest of my breath.

"Murphy's not interrupting this," he said, voice low and certain.

I barely had time to register the words before he crossed the space between us.

His hands found my waist and backed me against the door. Then his mouth was on mine again—deeper and more insistent, all restraint slipping.

The pressure at my waist grew stronger. Then his mouth slowed. He drew back gradually, like it took effort to separate from me.

"You have no idea…" His voice faded as his gaze drifted from my face to my shoulders, to the straps of my dress.

My pulse thudded. His hands drifted upward, slow and deliberate, until his fingers found the buttons at the front of my dress.

He loosened one. Then another, working them slowly open, his gaze never leaving mine.

When the fabric fell loose, he tucked his thumbs underneath the straps and eased them down until they slipped off my shoulders. The dress pooled at my feet.

"I can't believe you're real." He met my eyes, something softer moving through them. "And you're here."

I saw the faintest tremor in his hand when he reached up to brush my hair back from my face.

I covered it with mine.

His jaw tightened slightly.

"Jess," he said again, softer this time.

"I'm here," I whispered.

His mouth found mine again—slower, deeper—and as he kissed me, he walked me backward until the backs of my knees met the mattress. I sat, leaning back on my hands.

He didn't follow. He stayed there, letting his gaze roam over me, slow and deliberate.

Heat curled low in my stomach.

"Are you just going to stand there?" I asked softly.

His mouth twitched. "I thought I might."

I let my gaze drop to the hem of his T-shirt.

"Would you at least take your shirt off?"

His eyes darkened as he reached for the back of his collar and pulled his T-shirt over his head.

"Since you asked so nicely," he said as he tossed it on the floor.

My breath caught. I'd seen flashes of his abdomen— quick moments, accidental glimpses.

This wasn't that.

This was mine.

The bed dipped as he settled beside me.

"You okay?" he asked quietly.

Instead of answering, I reached out and pulled him down to me.

His mouth pressed against mine again. Deliberate. Then it deepened fast, his hand sliding into my hair as he tilted my head and took control of the angle.

My hands slid down his back, fingertips grazing warm skin before curling into him, pulling him closer.

I followed his lead.

When he kissed me harder, I met him there. When he shifted, I moved with him, my hands tracing warm skin and muscle, mapping him by touch instead of sight.

A soft sound escaped me when he finally pulled back, but it barely lasted a second before his mouth dipped lower.

His lips followed the curve of my throat, finding the place where my pulse beat hardest. I tilted my head without thinking, giving him access, and something in his expression told me he knew exactly what he was doing.

He lingered there a moment before dragging his mouth back up—over my jaw, along my cheek—until his breath brushed my ear.

"You're so sweet." His tongue traced the delicate curve before his teeth closed gently around the lobe and tugged, pulling a soft sound from me.

Goosebumps rippled over my skin. Caleb must have felt the change because he stilled, and his gaze drifted downward.

The look in his eyes changed.

His hand slid upward, brushing over the lace of my bra before settling there, warm and sure. Heat spiked through me when his thumb found the peak beneath the lace.

I felt his warm breath against me a split second before his mouth closed over the lace, his tongue tracing slow circles while his thumb echoed the motion on the other side.

My hands flew to his shoulders, gripping hard because if I didn't anchor myself to something solid, I was pretty sure I'd dissolve right there.

He moved between them, relentless, until I was trembling beneath him, fingers twisted in the sheets.

Caleb pulled back and looked down at his handiwork,

and his mouth curled into a satisfied smile. I followed his gaze and saw my nipples pressing forward through the thin lace.

His hand slid behind me, and I arched when he released the clasp. He drew the straps slowly down my arms before easing the lace away.

"God, Jess…"

He touched me again, thumbs circling my nipples before pinching them and tugging gently. I swear, I almost came on the spot.

"Caleb…" His name came out on a hoarse gasp.

He dipped his head and dragged his open mouth down my belly, nipping at the waistband of my panties before catching the fabric in his teeth and tugging. His hands followed, and seconds later I was lying there, completely naked.

I should have felt nervous. Exposed.

But I didn't.

Not with him.

The way he was looking at me didn't make me want to cover myself. It made me want to hold his gaze and let him see everything.

He shifted onto his stomach and settled between my thighs.

For a second, he just looked at me—at all of me—before his gaze lifted and met mine across the length of my body.

"Watch," he said, his voice low and steady.

I didn't look away.

When he dipped his head, I knew what was coming.

I just hadn't expected it to feel like that.

His tongue dragged through me before circling my clit. He varied the pressure, changed the pace, until I couldn't tell where one sensation ended and the next began.

My hips arched, pressing against his mouth.

"Oh, God." I didn't recognize my own voice.

His hands pressed against my stomach, holding me in place. Not restraining, just steadying.

"I've got you," he said.

He lingered, his warm breath brushing my sensitive skin. That single second of anticipation nearly killed me. Then his mouth opened over me and he sucked. Over and over, slow and devastating, his tongue never quite letting me catch my breath.

My fingers found his hair, gripping as I watched his head move between my thighs. I'd never done that before—watched.

Never thought I'd want to.

But I couldn't look away. Not when he looked like that—like there was nowhere else he'd rather be.

He pulled back just enough to look up at me, his breath still warm against my skin. His finger moved over me slowly, a question and a promise at the same time.

"You okay?"

I nodded, panting.

"Good, because we're not nearly done here."

That was the only warning I had before his finger slipped inside. I felt stretched and sensitive, and every slow stroke made me grip him harder. His thumb brushed my clit once, then again, before settling into place and moving in slow circles.

Caleb's gaze shifted between my face and what he was doing, watching me like my reaction was the whole point. When he added a second finger, curling them just right, I stopped trying to think altogether.

I dug my fingers into his scalp and held on, surrendering to wherever he wanted to take me. Every stroke, every pull of his mouth wound me tighter until I was balanced on the edge.

Then he sucked hard, and I shattered.

When I could breathe again, he was beside me, just watching.

I took in a deep breath and let it out slowly.

"I think I just died."

"You didn't." Caleb pressed a kiss to my hip. "I checked your pulse."

"Oh, is that what you were doing?"

He traced slow circles on my stomach.

"Mm-hmm."

He moved back, and I couldn't miss the tent in his shorts. Instinctively, I reached for it.

Wrapping his fingers around my wrist, he stopped me before I made contact.

"Next time, okay?" He flashed a pained smile. "I'm hanging on by a thread here."

"Good to know." I smiled. "Do you have a condom?"

He was off the bed before I finished the sentence.

I watched him rifle through the bedside drawer. After a few seconds, he straightened and held up a condom like a victory trophy.

After tossing it on the bed, he slipped his thumbs into the waistband of his shorts and pulled them and his under-wear down in one swipe. He straightened, and I felt my jaw drop.

"Oh, wow."

He looked around.

"What?"

"You're..." I swallowed. "Just wow."

He kneeled on the bed and leaned down to give me a quick kiss.

"Oh, yeah?" he asked against my mouth.

"Yeah." I smiled as he straightened.

He tore open the condom packet, and I watched, fascinated, as he rolled it down every inch of him. Of which there were many.

That done, he met my gaze and settled between my thighs.

Reaching down, he lined himself up with my entrance and pushed forward, sinking into me in one long thrust. The sound I made was somewhere between a gasp and a groan.

He stayed still, giving me a moment to adjust, and I exhaled slowly as my body stretched to accommodate him.

"Damn." The word sounded more like a prayer than a curse. "You feel so good." He pulled back and slowly thrust forward and stilled again. His jaw tightened. "I'm gonna apologize in advance...this isn't gonna last very long." He circled his hips and pulled back. "But I swear I'll make it up to you next time."

He pushed forward again, this time keeping a slow, steady rhythm. My body gripped him with every thrust, and I braced my feet against the bed as he picked up the pace, pressing my hips up to meet him. With each thrust, he nudged against my clit, and I wrapped my legs around his waist, wanting more.

"Christ, Jess. You're driving me crazy."

His thrusts got harder, faster, almost frantic. And then he hit *that spot*. Over and over, until I let out a long, low groan and shattered around him.

Caleb gripped my hips and slammed into me twice more before a low growl tore from his throat, and he collapsed against my chest.

He stayed there for a moment, breathing hard against my skin, his weight heavy and solid on top of me.

Then he lifted his head and brushed his mouth over mine, slow and lingering.

"You okay?" he asked quietly.

I nodded.

He pressed his forehead to mine before rolling off the bed. I heard the rustle of tissue, the soft murmur of the bathroom faucet.

When he came back, he didn't say anything. Just slid in beside me and pulled me against his chest.

I drifted off to sleep listening to the steady beat of his heart.

caleb

THE LIGHT WAS TOO BRIGHT.

I opened my eyes and blinked, then reached for my phone to check the time.

9:07.

I stared at it for a second.

Nine?

On a weekday, Murphy usually started pacing if I wasn't up and about at 6:15 sharp. Saturdays, he'd stretch it to seven if I was lucky. Sunday wasn't much different. He liked his routine, and honestly so did I.

But the house was quiet.

No nails clicking on hardwood. No dramatic sighs meant to guilt me out of bed.

I turned my head slowly toward the door.

Still cracked open from last night.

He's a pretty smart dog. He must have decided that Jess being in my bed was more important than his breakfast schedule.

And he wouldn't be wrong.

I looked down, and my mouth curved into a slow smile.

Jess was curled into me, one leg thrown over mine, one arm tucked between us, with her hand resting flat against my chest like she'd claimed the spot sometime in the night and had never given it back.

My brain went quiet.

Her hair was a mess—half across my shoulder, half covering her face.

Mine.

The thought landed heavy and sure.

I didn't move, and didn't want to.

Last night flashed through my mind in pieces. Her eyes when I told her to watch. The way she didn't look away. The sound she'd made when she came. The way she'd pressed into me afterward like she trusted me to hold her there.

I'd meant it when I said I had her.

Every second of it.

And lying here now, with her breathing slow and even against my ribs, I felt that same steadiness settle into place.

I'd known from the start that this wasn't casual or something I'd wake up and second-guess.

This thing with Jess was different from the start. There hadn't been fireworks. It had been steady. Slow.

So slow I hadn't seen it happening.

And by the time I finally did, I was already halfway in love with her.

Jess shifted slightly, her fingers curling into my chest. I slid my hand up her back, slow and careful, and let it rest between her shoulder blades.

Her eyelashes fluttered once before she looked up at me, disoriented for a second. Then she registered where she was. And who she was with.

Her mouth softened.

"Morning," she murmured, her voice thick with sleep.

"Morning."

"You're still here," she said quietly.

That made me laugh.

"Yeah. I live here."

She pressed her face into my chest, her chuckle muffled against my skin.

I brushed my thumb along her back. "You okay?"

She nodded and settled back into her original spot.

"Yeah," she said. "I just...didn't know if last night was a dream."

I kissed the top of her head.

"It wasn't."

She went quiet again, and I let the moment stretch.

But Murphy would only be patient for so long.

"I've gotta go let Murphy out," I said.

She made a small protesting sound but didn't let go immediately.

"Five minutes," she muttered.

"You're negotiating on no caffeine," I said.

Her lips curved faintly.

"Come back," she added, softer.

"I will."

This time, when I eased out from under her, she rolled onto her side, curling into the warm space I left behind.

I slipped into my shorts, and before leaving the room, I grabbed a clean T-shirt from my dresser and laid it at the foot of the bed where she'd see it. Just in case.

Murphy was lying at the bottom of the stairs, head resting between his paws.

"Thanks, Buddy," I said as I reached the bottom. "I owe you one."

He stood, and I scratched behind his ears before nudging him toward the back door.

Tail wagging, he trotted outside, and I leaned against the doorframe, breathing in the morning air.

Last night hadn't changed everything.

But it had changed something for sure.

And for the first time in a long time, I didn't feel the need to analyze it to death.

It just felt...right.

After Murphy did his business, we headed back inside. I heard the soft creak of the stairs and turned.

Jess stood there in my T-shirt, barefoot, hair still wild.

And my chest did that thing again.

The fabric swallowed her a little, and the hem landed just above her knees.

I'd seen her dressed up. Confident. Put together.

But something about seeing her in my clothes, standing in my kitchen, hit harder than all of that.

She reached down and petted Murphy. He tipped his head back and gave her that full, tongue-out smile he saves for his favorite people.

"You're so handsome," she said with a smile, then leaned down and kissed the top of his head.

I chuckled. "Should I be jealous?"

She glanced down at Murphy, then back at me. "He's a close second, but you're definitely my favorite."

I crossed the kitchen in two steps and pulled her into my arms.

"Definitely?"

She nodded. "Definitely."

I bent and brushed my mouth over hers.

It was meant to be a quick kiss. It wasn't.

Her hands slid up my chest, and I backed her gently into

the counter, my mouth deepening against hers before I could stop it.

When we finally pulled apart, both of us breathing a little harder than necessary, her stomach growled. Loudly.

She froze.

I blinked once. Then I laughed.

"Well, I was going to ask if you're hungry," I said, brushing my thumb along her cheek. "But I guess that answers that."

"French toast or pancakes?" I asked.

"French toast," she said. "But I'm not just sitting there while you do all the work."

I grabbed eggs and milk from the fridge and set them on the counter.

"Mixing bowls are in there."

I pointed to the cabinet above her head and reached for the bread.

She rose up on her tiptoes to pull down a blue bowl, the hem of my T-shirt riding higher on her thighs.

Watching her move around my kitchen like she belonged there made it hard to imagine her anywhere else.

Yeah. I could get used to this.

CHAPTER THIRTY-ONE

CALEB KNOCKED TWICE and let himself in just like he'd been doing the past week. I looked up from the proposal I'd been editing and smiled.

"You're early."

He dropped his keys on the counter but didn't return the smile.

"The Foundry's closed tonight," he said.

I straightened. "Closed? Why?"

He came around the couch and sat down, rubbing a hand over the back of his neck.

"Duncan passed this afternoon."

"Oh."

I hadn't known him well. We'd had a handful of quick conversations in the hallways. A thank you when he'd told me he liked what I'd done with my balcony plants. A smile when I'd signed my lease.

But The Lochwell was Duncan.

The renovated brewery. The apartments. The businesses downstairs. The way the whole place felt like history and fresh paint at the same time.

It was all his.

"When?" I asked quietly.

"This morning. He had a heart attack," he said, then added, "Lou said it was quick."

I nodded, absorbing that.

"That's awful," I said. "But I'm glad he didn't suffer."

I set my laptop on the coffee table and turned toward him.

Caleb shifted closer without thinking about it, his arm sliding around my shoulders.

"Yeah," he said. "Me too."

"Are we still meeting your friends?" I asked.

"They moved it to the Moosehead instead."

"Sounds good."

"I have to warn you..." he pulled back to look at me. "It's karaoke night."

"Too bad my mom's not here. She loves karaoke."

"How about you?"

"I've been known to sing on occasion," I said. "But I don't think the first time I'm meeting your friends should be one of those occasions."

"After two beers, at least one of them will think he's a country singer."

I laughed and settled back against him, wrapping my arm around his waist. "Are you done for the day?"

He nodded against my hair. "I had a meeting with Carli and my sales guy, but she cancelled once she got the news."

"When did you want to head out?"

"Whenever you can leave."

I sat and stretched my arms over my head. His eyes followed the movement.

"What?" Even though I knew. I just wanted to hear him say it.

"You're very distracting."

"So are you." I leaned down and kissed him—quick, but not entirely innocent. Straightening, I brushed my hand down his chest. "I'm just going to change. Then we can go."

An hour later, I was sitting on Caleb's deck while he showered upstairs. Murphy and I had played catch, and now he was lying in the grass soaking up the sun.

I pulled my phone from my pocket and hit FaceTime.

Mom answered on the second ring.

"Hi, sweetheart."

"Hi."

She tilted her head. "Where are you?"

"I'm at Caleb's."

Her eyebrows lifted. "Oh."

I rolled my eyes. "Don't start."

"I'm not starting. I'm observing."

"So," she said carefully. "That's going well?"

I didn't hesitate.

"Yeah," I said. "It really is."

She smiled at that, softer this time.

"You sound different."

"Different how?"

"Settled."

"Mom, it's been a few weeks. Don't start planning the wedding."

My dad leaned farther into the frame. "Just give me his full name, birthday, and social security number. I'll run a background check."

"Dad," I laughed. "I could walk into town and get a full background check on him from literally anyone."

"Ignore him," my mom said, rolling her eyes. "It's just nice to see you happy. And you know Brett was never my favorite, so this is even better."

We talked about Edinburgh—the rain, the lift being out again, the café my mom was currently obsessed with. For a few minutes, it felt like I was back there instead of in Caleb's backyard.

"You and Caleb should come visit," she said.

"Maybe."

"Ohhh. We got a maybe." She glanced at my dad. "That's practically a declaration of love."

Declaration of love.

We hadn't said it. But it didn't feel far away.

"Mom," I laughed. "I just said maybe."

"Which means you really like him."

I hesitated for half a second. Then, speaking softer than before, I said, "I do really like him."

"Well," she said, smiling, "we'd love to meet him."

"He's upstairs getting ready. He should be down in a minute if you want to say hi."

"Actually, I'm right here," Caleb said as he stepped out onto the deck.

My mom leaned sideways, squinting at the screen like she could catch a glimpse of him if she angled herself just right.

He sat and shifted closer to me. I angled my phone so he'd be in the frame.

"Mom, Dad—this is Caleb," I said. "Caleb, this is my mom and dad, Elaine and Mark."

"It's really nice to meet you, Mr. and Mrs. Harper."

"Please, call us Elaine and Mark," Mom said.

He nodded. "It's nice to meet you, Elaine. Mark."

They talked for a few minutes, and every so often my mom would widen her eyes at me or tilt her head in approval, like she thought she was being subtle.

Of course they loved him. My mom was smiling like a wish she'd never admit to making was coming true.

A minute later, my mom covered a yawn.

"Okay," I said, smiling. "It's definitely past your bedtime." I glanced at Caleb. "And we should probably get going."

"It was lovely to meet you, Caleb," my mom said.

"You too," he replied.

Once the screen went dark, Caleb shifted closer.

"I really like you too."

"Yeah?" I asked softly.

He pressed his nose to mine, his mouth curving.

"Mm-hmm."

Then his mouth brushed over mine, slow and unhurried, like he wasn't trying to prove anything—just confirm it.

He didn't move right away.

Neither did I.

"We should go," I murmured against his mouth.

"Yeah," he said, though his hand tightened at my waist for another second before he let me go.

Murphy barked once from the yard like he'd decided we'd lingered long enough.

I laughed and stepped back. "Okay. Tavern. Karaoke. Your friends."

"Still time to bail," he said.

"Not a chance."

The Moosehead Tavern was packed.

The kind of full that happens when a town doesn't know what else to do.

"Ward!"

The voice carried over the hum of conversation.

Caleb lifted his hand in acknowledgment without breaking stride. "That's them," he said.

I followed his gaze toward the back of the room, where long wooden tables had been pushed together. Three couples were already settled in, and two pitchers of beer were sweating in the middle of the table.

As we approached, a tall guy with dark hair leaned back in his chair and grinned.

"There he is."

"And there she is," the woman beside him added, her smile warm and curious.

Caleb's hand slid from mine to pull out a chair. I sat, and he took the seat beside me.

"Jess, this is Max and Brooke," he said, nodding toward the couple who'd spoken. He gestured around the table. "Joe and Caitlin. Mason and Kelsey." His arm came around my shoulders. "Everyone—this is Jess."

Max stood first, offering his hand. "Nice to finally meet you."

Joe gave a nod that felt more observant than suspicious. "Hey."

Mason lifted his glass. "Welcome to the chaos."

Brooke leaned across the table and gave me a quick hug before I had time to decide if I was a hug person. "We're glad you're here," she said quietly—like she meant it.

"Your eyes are gorgeous," Kelsey said.

"Oh. Thank you."

"We're so glad you're here," Caitlin said.

No one grilled me. No one sized me up.

They just made room.

Caleb filled two empty glasses from one of the pitchers —Lochwell Lager, of course. He handed one to me.

I hadn't even gotten a chance to take a sip when a man rang the bell at the bar and called for everyone's attention.

"Today, Maplemoor lost a piece of itself. Duncan Lochwell turned a brick building into something bigger. Jobs. Homes. A place that feels like ours. Some of us worked for him. Some of us rented from him. All of us drank his beer."

That earned a quiet ripple of laughter.

"He did right by this town and its people, and he did it without needing a spotlight. Let's take a minute."

The room went still.

After a long beat, he lifted his glass.

"To Duncan," he said.

"To Duncan," the room echoed.

A few seconds later, someone near the bar started singing *"Total Eclipse of the Heart,"* confident, if not entirely on key.

Conversation shifted after that.

Stories about Duncan. About the renovation. About the old brewery days.

Then Mason leaned back in his chair. "Wonder what's gonna happen to The Lochwell."

"What do you mean?" I asked.

Joe shrugged. "Duncan's wife passed years ago. His son too."

"There's a grandson," Brooke said. "Graeme."

"I remember him from school," Max said. "He was a couple years older than us."

"Does anyone even know where he is?" Kelsey asked.

Caleb shrugged. "He left town with his mom after his parents divorced. I think we were in middle school."

"Something like that," Mason agreed.

"So what happens now?" I asked.

"Depends who owns it, I guess," Joe said.

"Or someone sells it," Brooke added.

The idea lodged in my chest.

Sell it.

I glanced at Caleb.

He was already looking at me.

His thumb brushed lightly against my thigh under the table.

Grounding.

"I love my apartment," I said quietly.

"I know," he said.

And he did.

Later, when conversations split into smaller clusters, Caleb stayed connected to me—knee pressed to mine, hand warm on my leg, thumb tracing idle circles while he talked to Max about his work at The Lochwell.

I'd never had that before.

Not the steady presence. Not the quiet certainty of it.

At one point Brooke leaned toward me.

"So," she said with a grin. "He's different lately."

"Oh?"

"Happier."

Heat crept up my neck.

Caleb glanced over, catching the tail end of the conversation.

"She's not wrong," he said.

His smile was sweet and sure.

Around us, the conversation drifted back to Duncan and The Lochwell—to ownership and what-ifs and change.

I didn't know what would happen to the building.

But somewhere between Duncan's toast, Brooke's

smile, and Caleb's hand warm on my leg, the knot in my chest had loosened.

I thought about what my mom had said.

Settled.

She wasn't wrong.

caleb

I PULLED up in front of The Lochwell a few minutes before eight.

Before I turned off the engine, Jess came through the front doors carrying a foil-covered pan like she was transporting something fragile.

I got out of the truck to meet her halfway.

"What's that?" I asked.

She shifted it in her hands. "Maggie mentioned people sometimes bring snacks to volunteer days. I made brownies."

"You didn't have to."

She gave me that small, easy smile. "I wanted to."

I set the pan on the back seat and tucked it against my tool bag so it wouldn't slide. Then I gave it a small nudge, making sure it stayed put before closing the door.

She watched me for a second.

"You don't mess around," she said.

"Not with brownies."

I gave her a quick kiss, then stepped back and opened the passenger door for her. She climbed in, and I rounded the hood and slid behind the wheel. I started the engine and pulled out of the lot, heading toward town.

"So what are we doing today?" she asked.

"Couple things," I said. "Rebuilding the dugout benches. Sheetrock in the clubhouse. Fence along third base needs reinforcing. And we're hanging the new sponsor signs."

She nodded, taking it all in.

"Normal cleanup," I added. "Stuff that didn't get done last year."

"And the whole town just volunteers?"

"Not the *whole* town. But enough to get the job done."

"I'm happy to do whatever."

She glanced over her shoulder at the back seat.

"They're fine," I said.

"I know, but it doesn't hurt to check."

I turned past the elementary school, and the field came into view behind it. A few trucks were already parked along the fence line. Others were backed up near the dugout. Luke stood on his tailgate, handing down lumber.

Jess rested her elbows against the dashboard and took it all in.

"They're not messing around."

"Opening day's in two weeks," I said.

"Will everything get done today?"

"I think so." I killed the engine. "Ready?"

She smiled. "Let's do it."

We climbed out, gravel crunching under our shoes. I grabbed the brownies from the back seat, double-checking the foil before shutting the door.

Maggie spotted us from over by the clubhouse and started toward us, wiping her hands on her jeans.

"You made it!" she said to Jess.

"And she made brownies," I added, lifting the pan slightly.

Maggie's eyes lit up. "Excellent!"

We followed her to the folding tables set up near the bleachers, and I set the pan down.

Maggie peeled back the foil just enough to inspect them.

"Fudgy?" she asked.

"Of course," Jess said. "I'm not a monster."

Maggie nodded approvingly and covered them again like they were a shared secret.

Emily came out of the clubhouse carrying a clipboard.

"I'm glad you made it, Jess," she said, then turned to me. "You're on dugout duty."

"What do you need me to do?" Jess asked.

"Do you have any preferences?"

"Whatever you need."

She looked at her clipboard again. "The dugouts are covered—and trust me, you wouldn't want to deal with that crew anyway."

"Hey," I said.

"You know I'm right," she said, then continued talking to Jess. "You can help Maggie deep clean the kitchen or organize the equipment room."

"I'll clean the kitchen. Someone who actually knows baseball equipment should probably handle that."

"Ward!" Max called from the dugout. "Are you gonna just stand there looking pretty or come help?"

"Aww, you think I'm pretty?"

"Yeah, yeah," he said. "Grab my battery from the clubhouse and get over here."

"Give me a minute," I called back.

"See what I mean," Emily said. "Give it twenty minutes

and they'll either be busting ass or trying to outdo each other."

"You say that like it's a bad thing."

I turned to Jess. "You good?"

Jess nodded. "Yeah."

"We'll take care of her," Maggie added, already moving toward the clubhouse.

Jess fell into step beside her.

I followed them inside long enough to grab the battery off the counter near the storage shelves.

Jess glanced back at me.

"I'll see you in a bit," she said.

I gave her a quick kiss before heading out to the field.

Max and Luke were already arguing over a sheet of paper tacked to the dugout wall. Once I got closer, I saw it had measurements scrawled in pencil and a rough sketch of the framing layout.

"What's the debate?" I asked.

"Bench supports," Max said. "He thinks we need at least two more."

Luke snorted. "We do."

I'd participated in enough of these builds to know the arguing usually started when it didn't really matter. Worst case, a twelve-year-old sits on a bench that wouldn't collapse.

"What's the issue with putting in more?" I asked.

Max blinked at me.

"Fine." He jerked his chin toward Luke. "Grab a couple more brackets."

Then he looked back at me. "You can drill for the anchors."

Luke was already heading toward his truck.

I grabbed the hammer drill. I'd rather get it done than stand around debating it.

By the time Luke came back with the extra brackets, I had the holes drilled, and within a few minutes we had the first one anchored into the cinder block.

Max adjusted the spacing on the sketch and the arguing turned into actual progress.

More trucks rolled in as the morning stretched on. People filtered through the gate carrying coolers, ladders, extra lumber. Someone fired up a mower near the outfield fence. A couple of dads started hanging new sponsor signs along the backstop. Over by the third-base line, two high school kids were scraping old paint off the railings.

It settled into something steady after that.

The rhythm of drills and hammers. The low hum of conversation. Laughter carried from the outfield, where someone had decided music was necessary.

A handful of kids chased each other along the warning track, while others ran around the infield dodging piles of lumber like it was part of the game. One of them picked up a stray baseball and launched it toward the backstop.

I'd been one of them once.

Running around while the adults worked. Sneaking sodas from coolers. Pretending the dugout benches were major league.

Back then, it felt like it all just happened. Like fields fixed themselves. Now I knew better.

I wiped my hands on my jeans and glanced toward the clubhouse.

Through the open concession windows, I could see movement inside—Maggie cleaning the counter, Emily crossing behind her. And Jess working right alongside them.

She had her sleeves pushed up and a rag in her hand, standing on a step stool to reach the top shelf of the cabinets. She was talking while she worked, smiling at something Maggie said, completely at ease.

Not hovering.

Not waiting for me.

Just there.

Like she'd always been.

Something in my chest loosened.

This is what it was supposed to feel like.

Not dramatic.

Not fragile.

Just steady.

I picked up the next bracket and held it in place against the cinder block.

"Mark it," I said.

And we got back to work.

CHAPTER THIRTY-THREE

AFTER FINISHING the paragraph I'd been struggling with for the past hour, I checked the time. I had five minutes before I needed to head to The Brewhouse to meet Caleb for lunch. Opening my inbox, I answered a few emails before coming to one with the subject line

"Contributor Bonus Pool – Secured Projects."

I scanned the email, then read it again more carefully and downloaded the attachment. The number at the bottom of the page made me sit back in my chair. I closed my eyes and opened them again. Still there.

Picking up my phone, I texted my project manager, Jim Kowalski.

Is this email for real?

It looks legit.

Holy hell.

I grabbed my bag and headed out the door, smiling.

Caleb was outside when I got there, standing nearby

with his phone in his hand. He looked up the second I stepped onto the sidewalk.

His eyes narrowed slightly.

"What's going on? You're practically vibrating."

I rose up on my toes and kissed him. "Maybe I'm just happy to see you."

"As nice as that would be," he said, "I'm thinking there's something else."

I hooked my arm through his. "Let's go order, and I'll fill you in while we eat."

He studied me for half a second longer, then pulled the door open. "Okay, but if you explode before we sit down, that's on you."

Vee smiled when we walked in. "Hey you two."

"Hey," Caleb said. "Is there chicken chili today?"

"Not today. We have the usual chicken noodle and minestrone."

"You really should have chicken chili every day," he said.

"We've discussed this more times than I can count," Vee said with a smile.

"I know, but it's worth revisiting every once in a while."

Vee shook her head and chuckled. "What can I get you?"

He looked at me.

"I'll have a BLT on wheat and an unsweetened iced tea with lemon."

Caleb ordered a turkey BLT and a brownie.

We settled at a table by the window.

"Okay, so what has you smiling like that?"

"Right before I came down here, I got an email from HR." I shifted in my chair. "You know how the new corporation restructured when they acquired us?" He nodded.

"Titles shifted and the reporting chain changed, and I got moved under sales. Which I didn't love at first."

He lifted a brow. "And now?"

"They have a contributor bonus pool for secured projects that *everyone* on the sales team gets a piece of. Including me."

"Wow! That's amazing."

"Right?" I found the attachment on my phone and slid it across the table.

He looked at the screen for a second before letting out a low whistle.

"You'll get that on every project you win?"

"I get a quarter percent of the project total for proposals I've written," I said. "It doesn't sound like a lot, but with the size of the projects, it adds up."

He looked at the number again.

Before he could comment, Vee told us our orders were ready. He got up to retrieve them and came back balancing both plates and drinks, clearly something he did all the time.

He took a long drink of water, then said, "That's incredible. You deserve every penny of it."

"I'm still a little in shock," I admitted as I picked up my sandwich and took a bite. "And it's not just the money—which, don't get me wrong, is *amazing*—it's nice to be recognized as a valuable part of the company."

"Jess, you are a valuable part. They wouldn't have even landed that last contract if you hadn't suggested restructuring the scope."

"Which I only felt confident enough to push for because you talked it through with me and confirmed it would work."

"We make a good team."

The way he said it wasn't casual. It wasn't teasing. It was certain.

Even after weeks together, that smile still landed somewhere low in my stomach. I took another bite, giving myself a second to breathe.

We finished eating and I pushed my plate aside.

"So my friends are coming next weekend," I said.

"Mmm." He took a bite of his sandwich.

"It's just Nicole and Brian, Maya and Jim, and Sasha and Justin. Tara and Henry are booked through the summer. So they'll have to come next time."

"That'll be fun."

"Are you ready to play tour guide?"

"Absolutely."

"And your first task is helping me figure out the logistics," I said. "My place only has two bedrooms. Back in college, we wouldn't have thought twice about cramming in wherever." I smiled. "But we're all a little more sophisticated now apparently."

"Apparently," he said, his mouth curving.

"So they looked into the B&B on Main Street, and that boutique hotel outside of town...I forget the name. Which is better?"

He set his glass down.

"Why doesn't everyone stay at my place?"

"Seriously?"

He nodded. "I have four bedrooms." He shrugged like it was nothing. "Problem solved."

I looked at him for a second.

"Are you sure?"

"Yeah," he said simply. "I'm sure."

caleb

MURPHY MET me at the door, tail wagging. I crouched down and rubbed his ears before straightening.

The house was already full.

Brian, Jim, and Justin were spread out in the living room, a college baseball game on in the background. Brian looked up when I walked in.

"Hey, man. Thanks for having us."

"Yeah, of course," I said. "How was your drive?"

A round of "good" and "no complaints" came back.

"Who's playing?" I nodded toward the TV.

"Florida and LSU," Justin said. "Third inning."

"Good game?"

"Getting there," Brian said.

"You guys need anything? Another beer?"

"I'm good," Jim said.

Brian and Justin said the same.

"All right. I'm gonna go see what Jess has planned."

"Good luck," Brian said. "They're debating dinner."

"Should be interesting."

I left them to it and continued through to the kitchen.

Jess looked up the second I walked in. "There he is."

I crossed to her and pressed a kiss to her temple. "Everything under control?"

"Mostly," she said. "We're trying to figure out dinner. Go out or stay in?"

"That's what I heard."

"Stay in," Brian called from the living room.

"Nobody asked you," Nicole called back.

"I'm going to shower and change," I said to Jess. "You can referee down here."

"What's your vote?" she asked.

"Nope, I'm Switzerland," I said.

"Convenient," Jess said.

I gave her a quick kiss.

"I'll be right down."

Upstairs, their voices softened to a low hum. I showered, and as I was getting dressed, Jess's laugh carried up the stairs.

It was strange how fast her being in my space had started feeling normal.

It just felt right.

I headed back down.

"What'd you decide?"

"Pizza and wings from the Moosehead," Jess said.

"Do I need to pick it up?"

"No, they're delivering." Jess set her wine glass down. "While we wait, why don't we talk about the agenda for the weekend?"

"Ooh, there's an agenda," Nicole said.

"Guys, get in here," Sasha said.

A minute later, they wandered in, beers in hand, and settled around the island.

"Okay," Jess said. "Tomorrow we're doing a waterfall hike. We're all up for that, right?"

"As long as it's not too crazy hard," Maya said.

"It's about three miles round trip, but the trail is pretty even," I said.

"Sold," Maya said.

"And Sunday," Jess continued, "Caleb mentioned fishing or kayaking." She looked at Nicole, Maya, and Sasha. "But I know that's probably not your idea of a good time, so if we want to split up, the guys can do that and we'll figure something out on our own."

The women didn't even hesitate.

"Split up," Nicole said.

"Absolutely," Sasha agreed.

"Well that was easy," Jess said. "Where are my friends who usually bicker over things for hours before finally making a decision?"

Nicole wrapped Jess's arm around her shoulder and pulled her in for a side hug.

"We've matured, remember?"

While the women debated the finer points of their Sunday plans, I grabbed a round of beers from the fridge and leaned against the counter with the guys.

"So fishing," Justin said.

"I have a buddy with a boat on the lake I had in mind," I said. "I figured I'd see if we can borrow it."

Brian looked up. "That'd be great."

"I'll text him and confirm."

"What time would we be heading out?" Jim asked.

"Early. No later than six," I said. "It takes about a half hour to get there."

He winced.

"Oh, suck it up," Brian said. "It's one day."

"Easy for you to say," Jim muttered. "You're a morning person."

"No we're not," Justin said. "We're adults who don't require twelve hours of sleep."

I figured this would go on for a while, but Jim just considered that, then shrugged.

"Fair enough."

The doorbell rang. I grabbed my wallet and headed to the door, paid the delivery guy, and brought everything to the counter.

By the time I set the boxes down in the dining room, Jess was following me with plates, napkins, and a bottle of wine.

"Does anyone need anything else?" she asked. "Water? Another beer?"

A round of responses came back and she handled all of it without missing a beat.

Within a few minutes, we were all seated around the dining room table. When Nicole saw the spread, her eyes went wide.

"This is excessive."

"I know," Jess said. "You're welcome."

Dinner blurred into easy laughter and too many wings. At some point, the game pulled half of them back into the living room, while the rest of the group lingered at the table with refilled glasses and plans for the next day's hike.

By the time the boxes were empty and the wine was gone, everyone settled into that comfortable, overfed tired.

Eventually the yawns started.

Maya and Jim were the first to head up to bed, then everyone else quickly followed.

Jess and I did a quick pass through the kitchen—sliding

leftovers into the fridge, loading the dishwasher, then turning off lights.

"Go ahead up," I said. "I'll let Murphy out and be right there."

She pressed a quick kiss to my jaw and headed toward the stairs.

"Don't be long," she said over her shoulder.

Murphy was already waiting by the back door.

I let him out and leaned against the doorframe, breathing in the night air for a minute. The yard was dark and quiet. Inside, the dishwasher hummed.

It had been a good night.

Murphy trotted back in a few minutes later, did a lap around the kitchen, and headed for his bed in the living room.

I turned off the last light and headed upstairs.

The bedroom door was closed but not latched. I pushed it open.

The lamp on the nightstand was on, casting the room in a warm low light. Jess sat on the edge of the bed watching me walk in, wearing my T-shirt and not much else.

She didn't say anything. Didn't need to.

When I crossed to her, she stood, hands sliding up my chest before she rose on her toes and pressed her mouth to mine.

I kissed her back, then pulled away just enough to say, "Your friends are here. You'll have to be quiet."

She looked up at me, and the corner of her mouth curved.

"I'm not the one who's going to need to be quiet," she said.

Before I could respond, her hands dropped to my waistband.

She held my gaze as she undid the button and slowly unzipped me, then slid her hands into the waistband and dropped to her knees, taking my jeans and boxer briefs with her.

Looking up at me through her eyelashes, she smirked.

"You'll want to keep it down," she said softly.

Before I could comment, she wrapped her hand around me, leaning forward slowly, teasing, coaxing, driving me wild. Every inch she took made it harder to think, harder to hold back. When she found her rhythm, I groaned, my fingers digging into the sheets as I fought to stay in control. She found a rhythm—slow, deliberate, frustratingly perfect—and every time I tried to move, she shifted just enough to remind me who was running things tonight. I wasn't going to last.

"Jess," I panted. "Stop."

Releasing me with a soft pop, she sat back on her heels. I reached forward and wrapped my hands around her waist, pulling her to stand. She came up easily, and I caught her mouth with mine. She opened for me immediately, her tongue sliding against mine, her hands gripping my shoulders like she needed the anchor.

I kissed her harder, and she made a soft sound against my mouth that did nothing to help my self-control.

When we finally pulled apart, we were both breathless.

For a second, everything stilled. Then her hands moved to my shirt, and I lifted my arms so she could pull it over my head. After that, she caught the hem of her shirt and drew it up in one smooth motion, revealing bare skin beneath.

My brain went offline for a second. Just long enough for her to press both hands flat against my chest and walk me backward until the backs of my knees hit the mattress.

I sat. She pushed me back against the pillows with one firm hand.

"Stay," she said.

She reached across me to the nightstand drawer, pulled out a condom, and tore it open without taking her eyes off mine. Then she rolled it on slowly, deliberately, like she had all the time in the world.

I was going to lose my mind.

She swung her leg over and settled over me, her hands braced on my chest.

"Quiet, remember?" she murmured.

And then she sank down and every coherent thought I had left the building.

She set the pace. Slow at first, frustratingly deliberate. Her hips rolled in a rhythm that made it very clear she was in no hurry. Every time I tried to take over, she pressed her hands flat against my chest and held me there. I stopped trying and just held on.

Her hair fell around us as she leaned forward and picked up the pace, her body gripping me with every movement until I was fisting the sheets and doing my absolute best to keep it together.

"Jess," I groaned.

"Shh," she whispered.

She kept moving, her rhythm building until I felt her start to unravel—the catch in her breath, the way her hands pressed harder into my chest. I held on until she shattered, and then I let go with her.

She collapsed against my chest, breathing hard, her hair spread across my shoulder.

We lay there for a long while, neither of us moving, the house completely still around us.

Finally I pressed a kiss to her temple and slipped out of bed to clean up.

When I came back, she was already curled on her side, eyes heavy.

I slid in behind her and pulled her close, her back warm against my chest.

She exhaled slowly.

"Today was a good day."

"Yeah." I kissed the back of her head. "It really was."

CHAPTER THIRTY-FIVE

CALEB HAD KISSED my shoulder in the dark before he left.

"You sure you don't want to come?" he'd whispered.

"I enjoy sleeping," I'd mumbled into the pillow.

He'd laughed quietly and pulled the blanket up around me before slipping out.

A few minutes later I heard low voices in the kitchen, the scrape of a chair, the back door opening and closing softly. Truck engines rumbled to life, then faded.

By the time I finally came downstairs, the house still felt like it was holding onto the early morning quiet.

Nicole was already awake, curled into the corner of the couch with a mug of coffee.

"They left at dawn," she said. "That's aggressive."

"Apparently that's when fish are vulnerable."

She snorted.

Maya wandered in from the hallway a minute later, running her hand along the wood trim as she passed. As an interior decorator, she noticed things most people walked right by.

"Okay," she said slowly. "This is solid."

"Caleb restored most of it himself," I said.

Maya crouched slightly to examine baseboards, then straightened and looked around the room with the kind of focused attention that meant she was actually assessing.

"Original millwork," she said. "And he kept it. Do you know how many people either rip this stuff out or paint it?"

"He loves this house," I said simply.

She nodded, still looking. "It shows."

I glanced around the room, seeing it through her eyes for a second.

For some reason, hearing her say that made me quietly proud. Like it reflected on him, and somehow on me, too.

The floors were wide planks, older than any of us, sanded down and sealed in a warmer tone than they'd probably been in decades. Caleb had told me he'd spent a week straight working on them after he bought the place.

The fireplace in the living room was brick. Simple. The mantle was darker than the rest of the trim because he'd rebuilt it himself last winter to match.

Nicole stood slowly and turned in a circle.

"This feels like he lives here," she said.

"He does live here," Sasha replied dryly.

"No," Nicole said. "I mean it feels chosen. Not temporary."

That landed somewhere deeper than I expected.

Because she was right.

Nothing about Caleb's house felt transitional.

It didn't feel like a starter home or a placeholder. It felt rooted. Intentionally kept. Intentionally improved.

And the strangest part was that I didn't feel like a guest in it.

I knew which cabinet held the extra mugs, that the drawer stuck if you pulled too fast, and the floorboard near the hallway that creaked unless you stepped wide.

Settling into someone else's life this easily should have felt dangerous.

Instead, it felt right.

After finishing our coffee, we got dressed and walked to The Brewhouse for breakfast.

The guys wouldn't be back until late afternoon at the earliest. Which meant we had the whole day and nowhere to be. Just us.

We'd all been together at the bachelorette weekend. And then the wedding a few weeks ago. But weddings are chaotic. You barely get five uninterrupted minutes with anyone.

This was different. Sitting at a corner table, with sunlight pouring through the windows and enough time to actually talk, used to be a typical Saturday. Now it needed to be carefully planned.

Nicole wrapped both hands around her mug and looked at me.

"Okay," she said. "We need the whole scoop."

"On what?" I asked.

Sasha gave me a look. "Don't."

I laughed. "What?"

"You know what," Maya said. "One minute Caleb is your fake date to Nicole's wedding, and the next we're all staying at his house for the weekend."

And there it was. I'd given them the broad strokes about Caleb and me, but I'd held back on the details. Not because I wasn't ready to talk about it. More like I was afraid that saying it all out loud to them would somehow jinx it.

They'd met him at the wedding. Danced with him. Seen him with his hand at the small of my back like it belonged there.

But this was normal life.

And normal life is where things either held or cracked.

"Jim liked him from the wedding," Maya said. "This weekend just confirmed it."

Sasha nodded, then added, "And he seems good for you."

Nicole tilted her head. "You seem...calmer."

"Is that code for boring?" I asked.

"It's code for settled."

That word again.

I stared down into my coffee.

"I am," I said.

Sasha's eyebrows lifted. "But?"

I sighed.

"There's no but."

Nicole just looked at me.

"Okay," I admitted. "There's a small one."

Maya smiled. "There always is."

"It's just...easy," I said. "With Brett, things felt good in the beginning too, and then I got blindsided."

Nicole's jaw tightened slightly.

"You were eighteen when you started dating Brett," she said gently. "And there were signs."

"I didn't see them."

"You ignored them."

"That's not better."

Sasha reached across the table and squeezed my wrist. "You were in love."

I nodded.

"I just don't feel like I'm negotiating with Caleb," I said

quietly. "I don't feel like I'm having to adjust myself to make things smoother."

"Did you feel like you were negotiating with Brett?" Maya asked.

"Little things. Subtle shifts," I admitted. "Sometimes I felt like I had to make myself smaller to avoid causing conflict. And I'm not just talking about my height," I added with a chuckle.

No one said anything for a moment.

"And now?" Nicole finally asked.

"Now I'm just...me."

"Does he make you feel like you're too much?" Sasha asked.

"No."

"Does he make you feel like you need to explain yourself?"

I thought about Caleb listening to me explain the bonus structure. The way he'd understood immediately.

"No."

Nicole leaned back.

"Then what's the fear?"

I stared at the table. "That it's too easy."

"That's not fear," she said gently. "That's unfamiliar."

That hit harder than I expected.

"With Brett, you were always bracing a little," she continued. "For the next conversation. The next compromise. The next adjustment."

I didn't want to admit that was true. But it was.

"With Caleb," she went on, "you're not bracing."

"The man is crazy about you," Sasha said. "That much is obvious."

Maya and Nicole nodded.

I exhaled slowly.

"It's still new," I said. "We've only been together a few weeks. It would be ridiculous to label it so soon."

The table went quiet.

"Whether you label it or not, it's still what it is," Nicole said.

She wasn't wrong about that.

caleb

WE HEARD the music before we even reached the bottom of the stairs.

A group of local musicians—guys who'd probably played every festival and fundraiser in Maplemoor for the last twenty years—were standing on stage, working through "The Weight" by The Band out in the courtyard, accompanied by half the crowd.

Duncan Lochwell's celebration of life was already full by the time Jess and I walked in.

The weather was sunny and warm, the kind of afternoon that made you want to stay outside until the light was completely gone. People were spread across the courtyard and out onto the grounds, coffee in some hands, beer in others.

It wasn't a service. It was a gathering of everyone who loved Duncan...which was pretty much the entire town.

Jess's fingers slipped into mine as we stepped off the last stair. She wore jeans and a soft pale blue blouse, sleeves pushed up like she'd dressed for a normal Saturday and not something heavier. Her hair was pulled back loosely, a few strands already escaping in the light breeze.

"Wow," she said quietly.

"Yeah."

My gaze moved across the courtyard.

Maggie stood near one of the long tables talking animatedly with Alexis. Emily had stationed herself behind the outdoor bar, even though she wasn't technically working, refilling glasses like she needed something to do with her hands. Vee had turned one of the picnic tables into a full coffee station—carafes from The Brewhouse, stacks of cups, creamers, sugar packets—because of course she had.

Jess squeezed my hand. "This is really nice."

"Duncan would've liked it."

Before I could say anything else, someone clapped me on the shoulder.

"You hear about the time he tried to install that tap line himself?" Mr. Halpern said, already halfway into the story.

Jess smiled. "No, but that sounds like it's going to end badly."

"Oh, it did," Mr. Halpern said. "Nearly flooded the whole place."

Before he could keep going, Pete Lawson wandered over with a beer in hand.

"You telling the tap line story again?" Pete asked.

"Best one there is," Mr. Halpern said.

Jess laughed.

At that moment Maggie caught her eye from across the courtyard and waved her over.

Jess glanced at me. "I'll be right back."

"Go," I said.

Maggie pulled her straight into whatever she and Alexis were talking about.

Pete shook his head. "Mr. Halpern's version leaves out the best part."

"Oh, yeah?" I said.

"Duncan blaming the pipe like it had personally betrayed him."

Mr. Halpern pointed at him. "Because it did."

Pete laughed. "Man stood there in ankle-deep water arguing with plumbing."

I didn't bother asking how that was the pipe's fault.

"That sounds about right," I said instead.

Pete and Mr. Halpern kept the stories going for a few more minutes before Tom Becker wandered over with his version of the same disaster.

That seemed to be how the afternoon worked.

One memory turned into another, and more people joined the circle every few minutes.

When the conversation shifted again, I eased out of the group and made my way through a handful of conversations—shaking hands, listening to stories about Duncan I'd heard a dozen times and a few I hadn't.

I found my parents near one of the long tables, my mom already deep in conversation with two of Duncan's longtime regulars while my dad nodded along like he'd heard the story before—which he probably had.

At some point, I grabbed a beer from the bar and leaned against one of the picnic tables, taking everything in. Jess stood with the book club near the far side. She glanced up, caught my eye, and smiled before turning back to the conversation.

Music drifted through the courtyard, voices layering over each other, and more people filtered in, settling into small clusters.

Before long, the space was packed. The band had

switched out at some point, and a Springsteen tribute group was working their way through "Rosalita." Kids chased each other between the tables while a second guitar kicked in on the chorus.

Jess found me somewhere in the middle of it.

"I just saw your parents," she said. "Looks like they're heading out."

"Yeah, they're gonna pick up Murphy on their way home."

"Does that mean you can stay the night?"

"If I'm welcome."

She answered by rising on her toes and pressing a quick kiss to my jaw.

"If you behave," she said.

"I can't make any promises."

I leaned down and kissed her, brief and easy, right there in the middle of the courtyard.

"You know Murphy's always welcome too. The Lochwell is pet-friendly. He could come hang out with me anytime. When you're working, or whatever."

"Yeah?"

"You know how much I love him," she said simply.

I took her hand and we drifted toward the drink table. Max and Joe were nearby, and we stood together for a while, the conversation easy and unhurried.

Late afternoon stretched into evening without anyone seeming to notice.

By eight o'clock, the courtyard was loud and warm, the kind of energy that builds when people have been drinking and swapping stories for hours. The band had taken a break, and a large white screen had been raised near the stage. Conversations quieted as the mayor stepped up to the microphone.

Before she started, I scanned the crowd and spotted Tessa, Margot, and Sylvie Bergmann near the stage. Their father Walter had bought Duncan's beer recipes decades ago. Walter had passed a couple of years back, and now his daughters were running Bergmann Brewing and reviving the Lagerheads, the MLB team their father had poured just as much of himself into. The fact that they'd shown up tonight felt like the right kind of full circle.

"Duncan believed this place should belong to everyone," Mayor O'Brien said. "When the brewery started struggling years ago, a lot of people would have buried their heads in the sand. Duncan didn't. He looked around, saw what Maplemoor needed, and pivoted."

She gestured toward the courtyard.

"He turned an old brewery into this—something bigger than beer. A place where people gather. Where friendships start. Where stories get told."

A few people nodded.

"He believed in stubborn dreams," she continued with a small smile. "And he believed a community should have a home. This place"—she motioned toward The Lochwell behind her—"was his way of making sure Maplemoor always had one."

"He wasn't always easy," she said with a chuckle, drawing a ripple of laughter. "But he believed in this town. And he believed in all of you."

Her gaze moved slowly over the crowd.

"The Lochwell stands as proof of what one stubborn dream can become, and what a community can build together."

She lifted her glass.

"To Duncan."

"To Duncan," the crowd answered.

Jess raised her glass beside me.

I swallowed hard.

"Before we turn the music back on," the mayor continued, "we wanted to share something."

The projector flickered to life.

Photos of Duncan filled the screen.

A few people laughed when a picture of him in a ridiculous Oktoberfest hat appeared. Others wiped their eyes.

The slideshow moved on—Duncan behind the bar at The Foundry, standing in front of the old brick wall during renovations, and another with half the town crammed around him at one festival or another.

Jess stood in front of me, leaning back against my chest. My arms rested over her shoulders while she loosely held my hands, her fingers tracing absentminded circles across my knuckles.

I covered her hand with mine.

The Lochwell glowed behind us.

Alive.

Rooted.

Steady.

And everything felt solid enough that nothing could possibly shake it.

CHAPTER THIRTY-SEVEN

IF SOMEONE HAD TOLD me a year ago that I'd be sitting inside The Iron Gate celebrating a five-figure bonus, I would've assumed they had the wrong Jess.

But here I was.

We'd held off until it opened—the old jail conversion we'd both worked on—to mark the occasion.

Caleb lifted his beer. "To the woman who just made more writing one proposal than I did selling three furnaces last winter."

I laughed. "That is absolutely not true."

"It feels true," he said, clinking his glass to mine. "And this is just the first of many."

We were seated at a table near the window. The sun was low but not gone, the sky still holding onto that soft May glow.

"I still can't believe it." I shook my head. "I've been writing proposals for eight years and never thought I'd get a piece of the pie beyond my salary. The sales guys made the big money on commissions. I was just..." I lifted my fingers in air quotes. "Admin."

He frowned. "You were never *just* admin."

"I know. But officially? That's how I was categorized."

"And now?"

I leaned back, letting the moment stretch. Letting myself enjoy it.

"Now I'm technically part of the sales strategy team," I said. "Apparently, the parent company has always been structured this way. If you help secure the project, you share in the upside."

"That makes sense."

"It does," I said quietly.

My first bonus had been in my last paycheck. Even though I knew it was coming, the amount still shocked me.

He reached across the table and squeezed my hand.

"I'm so happy for you."

I took a sip of wine and carefully set the glass down.

"It's not like I'm doing things differently now," I said. "I've always done the work. But this part is nice."

The waiter returned with our food, setting Caleb's burger and fries in front of him and the mushroom flatbread I'd ordered in front of me.

For a minute, we focused on our food.

Across the table, Caleb's gaze kept drifting around the room—up toward the exposed beams, along the old iron bars they'd worked into the design, over to a row of pendant lights hanging above the bar.

I smiled. "Are you checking the work?"

"Occupational hazard."

"How does it feel being here now that it's finished?" I asked. "Considering what a pain in the ass the project was."

He huffed a quiet laugh and leaned back in his chair.

"See that register?" he said, pointing at the ceiling with

a fry. "It took half a day to figure out how to get the duct around those beams."

I glanced up.

"Funny," I said. "On the drawings it looked easy."

"It always does."

He chuckled and popped the fry in his mouth.

I took a bite of flatbread and looked around as I chewed.

The space shouldn't have worked. An old county jail turned into somewhere people could come for date nights and craft beer. It should've felt gimmicky, but it didn't. The bones were too honest for that. You could still feel what the building had been, the weight of the stone, the deliberate heaviness of every door and hinge. Whoever made the design decisions had been smart enough to respect the history of the place. They'd just let it stand there alongside the pendant lights and the reclaimed wood menus.

I thought about the proposal I'd written. The scope documents. The site assessments. The energy load calculations I'd spent two weekends on. A stack of PDFs nobody outside the project team had ever read.

And here I was, eating mushroom flatbread inside it.

"What?" Caleb said.

I shook my head. "I'm just thinking about how weird it is to be inside something I only ever saw on paper."

He considered that for a second.

"Yeah," he said. "That must be pretty cool."

"It really is." I picked up my wine glass. "I love what I do. That might sound odd, but I really do."

Something in his expression softened.

"It doesn't seem odd at all," he said.

* * *

Murphy and I had met Caleb for lunch at The Brewhouse, then spent the better part of the afternoon outside. Me at one of the patio tables with my laptop, him wearing himself out at the dog park until his tongue was hanging sideways. It was only his second day staying with me, and so far he'd been an exceptional assistant. Quiet when I needed to focus, entertaining when I didn't.

The May sun had felt good for about two hours before it shifted, casting a glare that turned my screen into a mirror. So Murphy and I headed back upstairs.

Instead of sitting at my desk, I settled onto the couch. Murphy curled up beside me before I'd even opened my computer. For a while, the only sounds were his breathing and my keyboard. By the time I'd finished editing the Hendricks proposal, he was snoring.

Before signing off for the day, I checked my email. I answered the first two, and got excited when I saw the third subject line, *Organizational Update—Strategy & Growth*. The last email like that was about the bonus.

As we continue to integrate our regional teams following our recent acquisitions, leadership has identified in-person collaboration as essential to building a unified strategy culture...

I skimmed.

...all senior strategy contributors will be expected to participate in a series of in-office integration sessions at our Rochester headquarters. The first session is mandatory and will take place...

I looked at the dates, then checked my calendar.

That's next week.

...effective the first of the year, in-office presence will become a standard expectation for all senior strategy roles.

After reading the entire thing again, I closed my laptop.

Beside me, Murphy stirred. He lifted his head, looked at me for a moment, then shifted and dropped his chin onto my lap.

I rested my hand on his ear and reached for my phone.

Turns out I wasn't the only one who'd gotten the email. Dana had called HR already. Marcus had forwarded it to his union rep. The general consensus was that the timeline was real, and the company wasn't bluffing.

By the time Caleb walked through the door, I knew exactly what I was dealing with.

caleb

MURPHY PUSHED past me the second I unlocked the door, did his usual lap through the living room, then stopped in the middle of the kitchen and looked at me like he expected an explanation.

"I know," I said.

I grabbed his food, measured it out, and set the bowl down. He ate slowly. None of the usual inhaling it before I could even stand back up.

I changed and came back downstairs to find him on his bed in the corner, head between his paws, not sleeping. Just lying there.

I opened the back door.

He lifted his head, looked at the deck, looked at me, then put his chin back down.

"Seriously?"

He closed his eyes.

"Okay then," I said. "I'm going to take a shower."

He didn't move.

So I headed upstairs, stripped off my uniform, turned

on the shower, and stepped in before it had a chance to warm up. The cold hit my chest and I stood there anyway.

Rochester.

Four hours away. Five with weekend traffic.

Permanent.

I turned up the heat and stood there while the water ran warm, then hot, then too hot, and still didn't move.

Murphy was still on his bed when I came downstairs. I grabbed a beer from the fridge and settled onto the couch.

He didn't move.

Usually he'd have claimed the other end by now.

I grabbed the remote and pulled up *Superstore*. It was usually good for a laugh, but tonight it played in the background while I thought about my conversation with Jess.

"It's your career."

"I'd never stand in your way."

"We could try long distance."

"Whatever's best for you."

Safe words. Reasonable words. The kind that don't ask anything of anyone.

She'd looked at me the whole time like she hoped for something else.

Murphy finally stood and padded over, nudging my hand.

He let out a long sigh.

I scratched behind his ears and took a long pull of my beer.

"I know," I said.

He hopped up onto the couch and settled against my leg.

One episode of the show ended and another began.

The house felt the same as it always did—same walls, same floors, same view out the back window.

It shouldn't feel different.

But it did.

Somehow, in a matter of weeks, Jess had worked her way into all of it. My bedroom smelled like her lotion. Her sweatshirt was on the hook by the door. A romance novel sat on her nightstand, face down, waiting for her to come back.

I kept coming back to the same moment. Her face when I said "whatever's best for you." Not hurt. Not angry.

Just quiet.

* * *

The sound of knocking woke me from a deep sleep. Murphy barked, hopped off the couch, and ran to the door.

I looked around, confused for a minute, then stretched my neck to work out the kinks. Grabbing my phone, I cringed at the time...11:30. I was supposed to be at The Lochwell at eight.

There were three missed calls from the office.

I fired off a text—something about being up all night and oversleeping—then set the phone face down.

The knocking came again.

I pushed myself off the couch and opened the door.

Emily didn't wait for me to open it all the way. She breezed past me into the living room, already talking.

"Jason said you were leaving the pipe bender on the porch." She stopped, crouching down to give Murphy a scratch. He wagged once. She stood up, looked at me, and whatever she was going to say next didn't make it out. "What's wrong?"

"You want coffee?"

I walked toward the kitchen and she followed.

"No. What happened?"

"Nothing," I said as I grabbed the coffee from the cabinet and started measuring out the grounds.

"*Caleb.*"

I kept my eyes on the coffee maker. "Her company wants her in the office in Rochester full time starting in January."

Emily didn't react right away.

"For how long?"

"Forever."

Silence stretched between us.

"That's...big," she finally said.

"Yeah."

"No wonder you look like shit."

"Thanks."

She leaned against the counter. "You okay?"

"Sure."

"You don't sound sure."

"It's her career. I'd never stand in her way."

"That's not what I asked."

I didn't answer.

Because what was I supposed to say? That the idea of her packing up and leaving felt like someone removing a load-bearing beam from my house? That every time I pictured The Lochwell without her there, something twisted in my gut?

Emily studied me for a second.

"Do you love her?"

I didn't answer fast enough.

"Caleb?"

"I haven't told her that."

"I didn't ask if you told her. I asked if you do."

"It doesn't matter right now."

"Why not?"

"Because if I say it now it looks like I'm trying to manip-ulate her into staying here."

Emily went quiet for a second.

"So you do."

I didn't answer.

"You should tell her."

"And say what? Stay because I love you?"

"Would you go with her?"

"She didn't ask."

"Answer the question."

"I don't know." I looked around the kitchen. At the island I'd built from reclaimed oak. The cabinets I'd hung myself, level by level, over the course of a summer. Every corner of this house had my hands in it. "I've never wanted to live anywhere else."

"I know," she said.

I let out a laugh, but there wasn't much behind it. "Rachel left. Now Jess."

Emily looked at me. "Jess hasn't left."

"She will."

She softened slightly. "But Rachel chose to leave. Jess doesn't want to."

That landed harder than I expected. Because she was right. Rachel wanted something else—a different life, a different pace, maybe a different kind of man. It wasn't about geography.

This was.

Jess wasn't running from Maplemoor. She was being pulled somewhere.

And that was worse.

"I don't know if I'd go," I said honestly.

"Because she didn't ask?"

"Because I don't know if she wants me to."

Emily leaned back.

"Or because if she doesn't ask, you don't have to decide?"

That one hit.

THE BREWHOUSE FELT LOUDER than usual.

Or maybe that's what happened after two days alone in my quiet apartment.

I almost didn't come to book club, but sulking in my apartment wasn't helping anything.

Maggie spotted me first. "There she is."

I forced a smile and sat down.

Emily looked at me with something that felt like sympathy, which meant she'd already talked to Caleb.

Maggie was talking about driving up to Penn State this weekend to bring her daughter home for the summer.

"You must be so excited," Alexis said. "My four drive me crazy, but I know I'll be a mess when they're gone."

"Don't remind me," Tiff said. "We just started the college search for the twins. I need a spreadsheet and a therapist."

The conversation moved around the table the way it always did. I nodded in the right places and laughed when everyone else laughed. I couldn't have told you what was said.

At some point it stopped.

"You okay?" Alexis said, looking at me over her mug.

I thought about brushing off the question, but I'd have to tell them eventually.

"You know how my company got acquired?"

"Oh, shit," Tiff said. "Did you lose your job?"

"No, nothing like that." I wrapped my hands around my mug. "I just got notice that I'll be required to work full-time in the office starting in January." I paused. "In Rochester."

The table went quiet.

"You're moving to Rochester?" Leeta asked.

Maggie frowned. "For how long?"

"It's a permanent relocation."

"That's a...big deal," Alexis said carefully.

"Yeah," I said on a sigh.

"How do you feel about it?" Maggie asked.

"Not great."

Ilona leaned forward. "Is there another option?"

"I could look for a new job, but the job market isn't great right now." I shrugged. "And with the benefits and bonuses I just started getting, that'd be crazy."

Emily finally spoke.

"And Caleb?"

There it was.

"He said it's my career. That he'd never stand in my way."

Maggie's mouth twitched.

"That's very Caleb."

"I know."

Understanding him didn't make it easier.

I wasn't angry at him. How could I be? He loved Maplemoor with a kind of steadiness that felt foundational. It wasn't stubborn or small. It was rooted.

And if I belonged to a place like that...I wouldn't leave either.

What was he supposed to say? It would've been ridiculous for him to beg me to stay. Just as ridiculous to offer to uproot his whole life—no matter how close we'd gotten.

So he said the only thing he could.

And somehow it still hurt.

"You love it here," Maggie said softly.

"I do."

The answer came easily.

I loved walking around town in the mornings. I loved that people said my name like I belonged here.

"So what are you going to do?" Alexis asked.

"Well, to start, I have to go to Rochester next week for some mandatory meetings. I'll find out more information then, but from what I understand, if I don't relocate, I'll lose my job."

Silence settled around the table.

"I know what you're all thinking," I said. "But Caleb and I have only been together a little over a month. Logically, I can't make a life decision based on that."

No one argued. How could they?

"Did you ask him to go with you?" Emily's tone made it obvious she knew the answer.

"I can't ask him to leave," I said. "His whole life is here. His family. His history. I'd never make him choose."

"And he hasn't offered?" Alexis asked carefully.

"No."

A quiet beat passed.

"What about long distance?" Tiff asked.

"Maybe." I shrugged, staring into my mug. "Rochester's only four or five hours away. People make that work."

But even as I said it, I was already poking holes in it.

Weekends only. Five hours each way. Something this new trying to survive that kind of distance before it even had a chance to grow.

Emily's jaw tightened slightly, but she didn't speak.

"I think," I said slowly, "if he wanted to leave, he would say it. And if he doesn't, that's okay."

"Is it?" Maggie asked gently.

I hesitated. "Yes."

Because it had to be.

I wasn't going to build a future on the unspoken hope that he might uproot himself.

And I wasn't going to sacrifice my career on the assumption that he wouldn't.

"But I don't have to decide anything just yet," I said finally.

"No," Maggie agreed. "You don't."

"But you do have to decide," Emily added softly.

caleb

JESS CAME over like she always did.

Like nothing had cracked.

Murphy lost his mind at the door, skidding across the hardwood as she stepped inside. She laughed automatically, dropping her bag and crouching to greet him.

It was so normal it hurt.

I stayed in the kitchen, watching her move through my house like she belonged there.

Because she did.

She stood, brushing her hands on her jeans. "We should talk."

I leaned back against the counter, arms crossing loosely over my chest.

"Okay."

She didn't ease into it.

"I can't do long distance."

The words didn't surprise me.

They just landed heavy.

"I know," I said.

Her brows pulled together slightly. "You know?"

"It wouldn't make sense. Not with something permanent like that."

She studied me carefully, like she was trying to read something deeper under the surface.

"And?"

"And what?"

"And what do you think about that?"

I shrugged. "It's your career."

Her jaw tightened just slightly. "Caleb."

"What?"

"You're not saying anything."

I dragged a hand through my hair and exhaled slowly. "I'm trying not to stand in your way."

"That's not what I'm asking you."

"Then what are you asking me?"

"Why does it feel like you're already stepping out of this?"

The question hit harder than I expected.

Because maybe I was.

The second she said Rochester, something in me had pulled back. Not out of anger or fear. Out of...self-preservation.

She'd be hours away permanently.

"I don't want you staying here because of me," I said finally.

"That's not what I asked."

"If you stay," I continued, ignoring that, "it has to be because it's what you want. Not because you feel tied to this."

"To you," she said quietly.

I didn't answer.

"To you," she repeated.

The kitchen felt smaller.

"I love Maplemoor," I said instead. "I've never wanted to live anywhere else."

"I know."

"And I'd never ask you to give up your future for me."

Her shoulders dropped slightly.

"I'm not asking you to ask me," she said. "I'm asking you how you feel."

I swallowed.

How did I feel?

Like someone had taken a crowbar to the foundation of my life and was asking if I minded. Like everything solid suddenly had an expiration date.

But if I said that—if I made it about me—then I was asking her to choose.

"You shouldn't give up your career because of me," I said instead.

She stared at me. "That's not the same thing."

"It's the honest thing."

"No," she said softly. "It's the safe thing."

That stung.

Maybe because she wasn't wrong.

"I'm not going to fight you on this," I said.

"I don't want you to fight me."

"Then what do you want?"

She hesitated, and for a second, I thought she might put it on the table and ask me. But she didn't. "I want to know we're standing in the same place," she said quietly.

I looked at her. "I'm right here."

She shook her head slightly. "No. You're bracing."

The word lodged somewhere under my ribs.

I didn't respond. Because I was.

If she left, I knew I'd survive. I had before.

But I wasn't going to beg someone to stay where they didn't want to be.

Even if it wrecked me.

Silence stretched between us.

"I can't feel like I'm the only one deciding," she said finally. "And I can't feel like I'm dragging you behind me either."

"You're not dragging me anywhere."

"That's the problem," she whispered.

The air felt thick.

"I don't know what you want from me," I said.

She held my gaze. "I want you to tell me you don't want me to go."

The honesty of it hit hard.

And I could have said it.

The words were right there.

Don't go.

Stay.

Choose us.

Choose me.

But the second I said them, they would come with weight. Obligation. Sacrifice.

And I couldn't live with the idea of her waking up five years from now wondering if she'd given something up because I asked her to.

So I didn't say it.

Instead, I said, "Whatever's best for you."

I watched it land, and saw something flicker behind her eyes.

Not anger or disappointment. Just...understanding.

Which somehow made it worse.

"Okay," she said quietly.

She stepped closer and rested her forehead against my chest.

"I love you," she whispered.

The words cracked something open inside me. We'd never said them out loud before.

"I love you too."

That part was easy.

Knowing what to do with it wasn't.

I'd meant it. Every syllable. And it still wasn't enough to make me say the other thing.

She stepped back first.

"Maybe we need some space," she said.

Space. A polite word for fracture.

I nodded.

"Okay."

She grabbed her bag and bent to kiss Murphy's head.

When the door closed behind her, the house felt too big. Too quiet.

I stood there for a long time.

Didn't move. Didn't argue. Didn't chase.

Telling myself I'd done the right thing.

I hadn't stood in her way or made it about me.

But as the silence settled in, one thought kept circling back.

Maybe not standing in her way wasn't the same thing as standing with her.

I just didn't know what else to do.

CHAPTER FORTY-ONE

I WASN'T GOING.

I stared at the clock on my stove.

7:02 p.m.

Book club started two minutes ago.

I'd been back from Rochester since Saturday. You'd think four days would be enough to get my head straight. But it wasn't.

What annoyed me most was that I couldn't seem to pull myself together. When Brett and I ended, I'd been devastated, but we'd been together eleven years. It shouldn't feel like this after a few weeks. But it did.

My phone buzzed.

You coming?

I answered Maggie before I could overthink it.

Not tonight. I wouldn't be good company.

The three dots appeared immediately, then disappeared.

I turned my phone face down and stared at the ceiling.

Twenty minutes later, there was a knock at my door.

I didn't move.

Another knock.

Maggie's voice came through the door. "Jess. Open up."

Of course they came to find me.

I pushed myself off the couch and went to let them in.

Maggie stood there holding a cardboard tray of coffees from The Brewhouse. Alexis had a white pastry box balanced on her hand. Emily was slightly behind them, arms folded loosely, her expression soft but knowing.

"What are you doing here?" I asked.

Maggie just said, "We told you. We show up."

My throat tightened.

I stepped back and let them in.

We ended up scattered across my living room—coffees in hand, shoes kicked off, pastry box open on the coffee table.

"So," Alexis said. "How was it?"

"It's a basic cube farm," I said. "The people seemed nice."

"But?" Maggie said.

"But I drove home through four and a half hours of nothing and sat in my apartment and cried."

No one said anything for a moment.

"You've built a life here," Alexis said quietly.

"You're not just visiting anymore," Maggie added.

That landed.

They weren't wrong. I'd built routines. Hikes. Mornings at the coffee shop. Book club. A rhythm.

"Have you talked to Caleb?" Maggie asked.

"We've been giving each other space."

Emily watched me over the rim of her cup but didn't say anything.

"Is there any way around it?" Alexis asked. "The relocation?"

"Not if I want to keep my job."

"So you're definitely going," Emily said.

"I don't really have a choice."

"There's always a choice," she said.

I looked down at my coffee.

Emily probably knew what Caleb was thinking, but I wasn't going to ask and put her in the middle of us. Eventually he and I would talk. Even if it was just to say goodbye.

"Okay," Maggie said. "We didn't come here to make you feel worse." She nudged the pastry box toward me. "Eat something."

Emily mentioned she and Jason were taking the kids to visit her sister Nora outside DC next month. Museums, the monuments, and a few days just wandering around.

"Tell her I said hi," I said. "I really liked her."

"She liked you too," Emily said. "She asked about you actually."

That was unexpectedly warm.

After about an hour, they gathered their empty cups and stood. Maggie squeezed my shoulder on her way out. Alexis pulled me into a hug that lasted a beat longer than necessary.

Emily lingered.

"I'm Caleb's sister," she said quietly. "But I'm also your friend. There's no right or wrong here." She paused. "I just want you both to be okay."

I nodded.

"You're not alone," she added.

"Thanks."

When the door shut behind them, I felt steadier.

Still broken. But steadier.

I sat there for a while, staring at the ceiling. My thoughts kept circling back to Caleb in his kitchen, arms crossed, saying all the right things in all the wrong ways.

Which was the problem.

We were both protecting each other.

And in doing that, we were building walls.

My phone sat on the coffee table, right where I'd left it.

Sometimes you just needed your mom.

I reached for it and checked the time—7:15 p.m. Just after midnight in Scotland. She'd definitely be asleep.

I hit FaceTime anyway.

It rang longer than usual.

Then her face appeared, barely visible in the dark.

"Jess?" Her voice was thick with sleep but she was fully alert in half a second.

"What's wrong?"

"Nothing's wrong," I said. "I just—" I stopped. "Everything's a mess."

She pushed herself upright and reached for the lamp. "Tell me."

So I did. I told her about the trip. The cube farm. The perfectly nice people. The four and a half hours home and the crying I couldn't seem to stop.

"And Caleb?" she asked.

"We're still giving each other space."

She was quiet for a moment.

"How's that going?"

"About as well as you'd expect."

"Jess."

"I know." I stared at the ceiling. "I know."

"Your father and I have been talking," she said carefully. "And I want to say something, but I don't want you to dismiss it before you actually think about it."

"That sounds ominous."

"Just listen."

"Okay."

"You keep talking about Rochester like it's the only option."

I frowned slightly. "For my job, it is."

"For *that* job," she corrected gently. "But not for what you actually do."

That made me pause.

"You respond to RFPs. You shape strategy," she continued. "You've been doing this for eight years, and you're good at it."

"Yeah?"

"Jess, municipalities outsource that kind of work all the time. Engineering firms hire consultants for proposals."

"But freelance isn't stable."

"I've been freelancing for twenty years."

"It's risky," I said.

"Yes," she said. "But so is uprooting yourself for a corporation that restructured once already and can do it again."

I exhaled slowly.

"I've always had stability and structure. A paycheck. A team."

She looked at me for a long moment.

"Your father moved us nine times," she said quietly. "You know I'd have followed him anywhere. But I also built something that was mine, something that stayed the same no matter where we landed." She paused. "You've found a place you want to stay. That's not nothing."

I sat up a little straighter, but didn't say anything.

"Come visit," she said finally. "Both of you. Whenever this settles."

After we hung up, I lay back on the couch.

Rochester. Maplemoor. Corporate structure. Freelance unknown. And Caleb.

For the first time since standing in his kitchen, it didn't feel like a wall closing in.

It felt like a crossroads.

Nothing was decided or fixed.

But maybe there was more than one way forward.

caleb

MURPHY JUMPED out of the truck the second I opened the door and trotted ahead of me up the porch steps, then stopped short.

Emily sat on the top stair, elbows on her knees like she'd been there a while.

Murphy's tail thumped once in recognition.

I paused at the bottom step.

"You know the door's open," I said.

She didn't move.

"I know," she replied evenly. "But I figured sitting on the porch waiting when you got home would be more dramatic."

Despite my mood, I smiled. "Mission accomplished."

Murphy leaned into her leg and accepted the ear scratch like it was owed to him.

"You gonna invite me in, or are we doing this out here?"

I climbed the rest of the steps and pushed the door open. Murphy went straight in.

"After you," I said to Emily.

She walked in and followed me to the kitchen. I filled Murphy's water bowl and grabbed two waters from the fridge. Emily leaned against the counter while I dropped my keys on the island.

"How's she?" I asked.

"She's holding it together," she said. "But she looks as awful as you."

"Have you talked to her about it?"

"I have."

"And?"

She leaned against the doorframe.

"And she's trying not to make it worse for you. Same as you're doing for her."

"Doesn't mean it's working," I said.

"No," Emily agreed. "It doesn't."

I exhaled slowly.

"This is her career," I said. "She's been there for eight years and just got access to that bonus structure. I'm not going to make her feel guilty for wanting to keep that."

"No one's asking you to."

"She shouldn't give it up."

"Caleb." Emily's voice was even. "Stop telling me what she should or shouldn't do and tell me what you want."

I didn't answer.

She waited.

"I want her to stay," I said finally. "But not because I asked her to."

"Why not?"

"Because if she stays for me and resents it later—"

"You're already deciding how she's going to feel," Emily said. "You don't get to do that."

That landed harder than I expected.

Murphy wandered back into the room and leaned against my leg.

"She loves it here, and she loves you," Emily said. "But she's been trying to make this easy for you, and you've been trying to make it easy for her, but in the middle of all that neither of you have actually said anything real."

I looked away.

"Tell her what you want," she said. "Not the safe version. The real one. Once that's out there, you two can figure the rest out together."

"And if what I want isn't possible?"

"Then you'll know. But right now you're both just standing in the dark."

The words settled.

Emily straightened.

"I'm not telling you what to decide," she said. "I'm just saying stop making it easy and start making it honest."

She opened the door and paused.

"And for the record," she added, "dramatic porch entrances only work once."

Then she was gone.

I walked into the living room and dropped onto the couch. Murphy followed and settled next to me.

He'd never needed a leash in Maplemoor. Not in this neighborhood, not on these streets or the trails. He knew the boundaries the same way I did—instinctively, without thinking.

In Rochester it would be different. Traffic. Noise. Sidewalks instead of yards.

But Jess would be there.

I reached for my laptop, logged on, and opened the company portal to the job openings.

There were two service tech positions available near Rochester. I clicked and read the descriptions. They were a little different from what I was doing now, but I could adjust.

Murphy rested his chin on my knee.

"You'll hate the snow," I muttered.

He licked my hand.

I opened a new email.

To: Mark Henderson

Subject: Transfer Inquiry

I stared at the blank body for a long moment, then typed.

Hey Mark,

Out of curiosity, what would the process look like for requesting a transfer to the Rochester branch?

I'm not making any decisions yet. Just trying to understand the logistics if it were ever something I considered.

Thanks,

Caleb

I read it once.

Twice.

It didn't feel dramatic or reckless.

It felt like acknowledging a door existed.

I hit send.

The house didn't shift.

The floors didn't creak differently.

Maplemoor didn't stop being home.

But for the first time in my life, it didn't feel like the only answer.

Turns out there was exactly one person who could make leaving feel like something other than a loss.

CHAPTER FORTY-THREE

CLARITY DOESN'T ALWAYS FEEL dramatic.

Sometimes it feels quiet.

After talking to my mom, I woke up feeling lighter, without that tight knot in my chest that had been constant since hearing about Rochester.

I wasn't relocating to Rochester.

Not because of Caleb.

Because I wanted to stay in Maplemoor.

I made coffee and opened my laptop, not to check corporate email, but to a blank spreadsheet.

Savings.

Monthly expenses.

Insurance.

If I finished out the year, I'd collect at least two more bonuses based on projects already in the pipeline. That alone would give me a nice cushion.

The twenty thousand I'd just earned sat in my account like proof.

That wasn't luck. That was skill.

And skill was portable.

I opened a blank document and started writing down what I actually knew how to do.

- **Proposal strategy.**
- **RFP responses.**
- **Project coordination.**
- **Lifecycle energy compliance.**
- **Grant language.**

The list kept growing.

For eight years, I'd thought of myself as the person behind the scenes—the one shaping proposals while someone else signed the contract.

Maybe that had been the wrong way to think about it.

I could do this.

Not recklessly.

Not tomorrow.

But I could build it alongside my current job.

I'd need to put feelers out. Reach out to engineering firms I'd worked with in the past and let them know I'd be available for consulting after December.

If something landed early? Even better.

I leaned back in my chair and looked around my apartment.

Morning light filtered through the windows, catching the little basil plant Maggie had insisted I keep alive on the sill. The Maplemoor Moose plushie I bought at the Legends & Lore Festival sat on the chair.

Maplemoor had been a fresh start, but it had become something better than that. It had become home.

The coffee shop. The trails. Book club nights that somehow turned into three-hour conversations. And best of all, Caleb.

And for the first time since Rochester entered the picture, the future didn't feel like something happening *to* me.

It felt like something I might actually get to build.

I wasn't ready to talk to Caleb yet. I needed to say it out loud to someone first—to hear how it sounded before I walked into that conversation with him.

I picked up my phone.

Do you have time to talk today?

Maggie texted right back.

Sure, I can meet you at The Brewhouse. Now?

How about if I come to you?

I'm home all day.

On my way.

* * *

Maggie opened the door with flour on her cheek and an amused look on her face. "You look like you've decided something."

"I have."

She stepped aside to let me in.

I paced once through her kitchen before I turned back to her. "I'm not relocating."

Her face broke into a smile. "Thank God." She pulled out a chair. "Sit. Tell me everything."

"I'm staying with my company through the end of the

year and collecting my salary and any bonuses from projects we win," I said. "While I'm doing that, I'm building a freelance consulting practice—proposal strategy, RFP development, grant writing. I'll be reaching out to firms I've worked with and searching online for leads."

"That's not a small move," she said.

"No, but I think it's the right one."

"Do you have a safety net?"

"I have savings. And my parents offered to help if I need it." I paused. "I won't take it, but knowing it's there is nice."

"You don't do things halfway."

"No."

She studied me for a second. "Does Caleb know?"

"Not yet."

"Why not?"

Because if he knows I'm staying, he might think it's for him. Because if he knows I'm building here, he might relax into that instead of engaging. Because if he hears it second-hand, it won't be a conversation.

"I'll talk to him," I said. "Not about Rochester. About us."

Maggie didn't interrupt.

"When it got hard, he shut down."

"And?"

"And I can't pretend that didn't happen."

She nodded once. "So what do you need?"

"I need him to show up," I said. "Not step aside. Not be noble. Not be quiet."

There it was.

The actual wound.

"It's not about whether he'd move or ask me to stay," I added. "It's about whether he's willing to say what he wants."

Maggie studied me carefully. "And what do you want?"

I didn't hesitate this time. "I want him."

The words didn't feel dramatic. They felt factual.

"But I don't want to be the only one choosing."

She crossed the room and squeezed my hand.

"You're not."

I wasn't sure that was true yet.

But I wanted it to be.

* * *

Back at my apartment, I sat with everything for a while.

Staying in Maplemoor didn't fix us. It didn't erase the way he'd gone quiet in the kitchen or the way I'd felt alone in that moment.

But it changed something else.

I wasn't cornered anymore. I wasn't reacting. I was choosing.

Tomorrow, I'd call him.

caleb

I ALMOST DIDN'T KNOCK.

For a full ten seconds, I stood there, staring at her door like it might open on its own and save me from having to do this part.

Murphy sat beside me, calm as ever, like this was just another Saturday and not the night I might lose the best thing that's ever happened to me.

In one hand, I had a small paper bag from The Brewhouse, grease already soaking through the bottom from the apple fritter inside. In the other, I held a tote from the historical society gift shop. I'd gone a little overboard with Maplemoor Moose merch. I got her a baseball cap, T-shirt, navy hoodie, keychain, and tumbler.

It had all felt right in the moment.

Now it felt like I was showing up to apologize with souvenirs.

I knocked anyway.

A second later, the door opened.

Jess stood there in leggings and a loose tank top, hair

pulled up into a messy bun. Her eyes were a little pink, like she'd been crying recently or hadn't slept well.

We just looked at each other.

"I brought you an apple fritter," I said, because apparently I was twelve.

Her gaze flicked to the bag in my hand. Then to the tote. Then back to my face.

"My favorite," she said softly.

That almost undid me.

"Can I come in?"

She hesitated for half a breath, then stepped back.

Murphy slipped inside like he'd been invited personally, tail wagging. Jess crouched briefly to give him a scratch before he made a beeline for the couch and jumped up like he owned the place.

Jess shut the door behind me.

I set everything on the kitchen table, suddenly hyper-aware of how quiet the apartment was. Neither of us sat.

"I'm sorry," I said.

No preamble. No explanation.

Her chin lifted slightly. She waited.

"I'm sorry I shut down on you." The words scraped on the way out. She swallowed but didn't interrupt.

"I told myself I was giving you space. That I didn't want to pressure you." I let out a breath.

She folded her arms, not defensive—just bracing.

"But I was protecting myself," I said. "If I acted like it didn't matter, then I wouldn't have to feel like I was about to lose you."

Something shifted in her expression.

I went on. "I've never once wanted to live anywhere else. But wanting you meant that might not be true anymore, and that scared the hell out of me."

The words landed between us.

I stepped closer, careful, like any sudden movement might break whatever was holding between us.

"You didn't deserve to be left standing there alone while I went quiet. I don't get to disappear when things get hard. Not with you." My voice roughened. "I won't do that again."

Her lips parted slightly.

"I can't promise I'll never be scared," I said. "But I can promise I won't shut you out. I won't leave you hanging like that ever again."

The silence stretched.

"I talked to my manager," I said, because this was the part that mattered. "There are openings in Rochester. It's not a done deal. I haven't applied or anything. But it's possible."

Her breath caught.

"I want to go to Rochester with you," I said carefully, "if you'll have me."

The words felt enormous.

Terrifying.

Freeing.

"I don't want you to choose your career over me," I added quickly. "And I don't want you to stay because you feel like you owe me something. I just...I love you. And I should've said all this a lot sooner."

There it was.

No polish. No strategy.

Just the truth.

Her hand came up to her mouth.

"I love you," I said again, softer this time.

For a second, she just stared at me.

Then she stepped closer.

"I'm not going," she said.

My brain lagged behind the words.

"What?"

"I'm not moving to Rochester."

Relief hit so hard it almost knocked me sideways—but she kept going.

"Not because of you," she said quickly. "Not only because of you. I've been thinking. Talking. Planning."

"Planning?"

"I'm going freelance," she said. "I've already started outlining a website. I have savings. I just got that bonus. I can stay through the end of the year at my current job while I build something on the side. If it doesn't work, I'll pivot. But I want to try."

She was talking faster now, like she'd been holding it in for days and couldn't get it out quickly enough.

"I love Maplemoor," she said. "The book club, the trails, the festivals." A small, shaky laugh escaped her. "I don't want to give that up for a corporate decision made in some boardroom."

My chest tightened.

"Staying isn't enough on its own," she said. "It's not about geography, it's about us. And if we're doing this, we have to do it together. Not half-in or scared."

I stepped into her space.

"I'm all in," I said.

Her eyes searched mine like she was looking for hesitation.

I held her gaze.

The corner of her mouth lifted just slightly before the tears came.

Mine weren't far behind.

"I love you," she said.

The words hit deeper than anything else had tonight.

I pulled her into me.

She came willingly, arms sliding around my waist like she'd been waiting to do exactly that.

We just stood there.

Breathing.

Holding each other.

Foreheads pressed together.

Murphy huffed from the couch like we were taking too long.

Jess laughed against my mouth as I kissed her.

Her fingers curled into my shirt. Mine slid into her hair. She made a small sound against my mouth, and I kissed her deeper, slower. Like I was finally saying everything I'd been too careful to say out loud.

When we finally pulled back, she rested her forehead against my chest.

"I thought I lost you," she whispered.

"You didn't," I said. "I just needed a minute to catch up."

She snorted quietly, then glanced at the table.

The apple fritter bag had tipped over, grease spreading into the wood grain. The tote with the moose merch leaned against the chair, half open.

"What did you buy?" she asked, voice thick.

"Everything," I admitted. "We can sell it later."

She laughed again—this time brighter.

"This town," she murmured.

"Our town," I corrected gently.

She looked up at me.

"Our town," she agreed.

I kissed her once more, softer this time.

And when she smiled against my mouth, I knew—staying wasn't standing still.

It was choosing.

And we had.

JESS

Three Months Later

I signed the contract at 9:12 a.m.

The exact time stuck because I'd stared at the "Accept" button for a full minute before clicking it, like the client might change their mind if I moved too fast.

When the confirmation email came through, my name sat at the bottom of the agreement in clean, black font.

Jess Harper. Consultant.

Not employee. Not admin. Not sales staff.

Consultant.

I let out a shaky laugh and pressed my hands against my cheeks, then flat against the desk to feel something solid.

Then I grabbed my phone.

I DID IT!!!

He called immediately.

"You signed?" I could hear the smile in Caleb's voice.

"Yes!"

He exhaled slowly. "I knew you would."

"I almost didn't."

"But you did."

"I almost threw up."

"That tracks."

I laughed and stood to pace because I didn't know where to put the energy.

"Dinner tonight," he said. "We're celebrating properly."

"I might still be in shock."

"That's okay. Shocked people still have to eat."

I smiled. "Okay. Dinner."

By 6:30, I'd changed outfits twice.

The navy dress won.

It wasn't dramatic. Just fitted enough to feel intentional. I slipped on my Jimmy Choo Azia sandals and checked my reflection one more time.

I wanted to mark the day somehow. Dinner with Caleb felt exactly right.

My phone buzzed just as I was fastening my earrings.

Can you meet me at The Brewhouse? Carli needs me to check something quick before dinner.

Sure. Be down in a minute.

The Brewhouse windows were dark when I walked up.

I hesitated, then pushed the door open.

The lights snapped on.

"Surprise!"

I actually stumbled backward.

Everyone from book club was there with their families. Caleb's family too. Even Nicole and the gang had made the trip from Philly. Around the room, several of Caleb's friends stood talking with their wives and kids.

I stood there for a second taking it all in. Then everyone started moving at once. Hugs, laughter, someone pressing a drink into my hand.

I stopped mid-hug when I noticed the setup in the corner.

"Is that a karaoke machine?"

"Luke," three people said simultaneously.

He held up his hands. "It's a celebration."

A banner was strung between two hooks above the counter.

CONGRATS ON YOUR FIRST CLIENT

And propped between two coffee canisters on the counter was an iPad. My mom and dad's faces filled the screen, both of them grinning like they'd been watching the whole thing unfold.

I looked from the iPad to the room full of people, still trying to process how any of this had come together.

"How?" I asked Caleb.

He pulled me into a hug before I could say anything else. I felt his laugh against my hair.

"You signed at nine twelve," he said when he pulled back. "That gave us plenty of time."

My vision blurred as I looked around the room.

"I can't believe you did all this."

He shrugged, but there was nothing casual about the way he looked at me. "Your first client seemed like something worth celebrating."

Nicole grabbed my hands, squeezing them like she might shake the reality into place. Alexis declared she'd always known I'd go rogue in the best way. Emily wrapped me in a warm hug that felt a lot like approval.

Maggie pulled me into a hug. When she stepped back, she squeezed my shoulders and said quietly, "You didn't just stay. You planted."

Planted.

When I finally caught my breath, I turned back toward the counter and leaned toward the iPad.

"You stayed awake for this?"

"Of course we did," my mom said brightly.

My dad nodded. "We weren't going to miss this."

It seemed like forever ago that I'd called my mom in the middle of the night, completely spiraling because I didn't know what to do.

She'd given me the best advice I could've asked for.

Tonight, they were watching me stand in the middle of The Brewhouse while people cheered.

The shift felt almost unreal.

In the corner, the tables had been pushed together just like they always were for book club, only now they held a full spread.

A cake with *Congratulations, Jess!* written across the top. Coffee carafes. Sandwich trays. Pizza. Pastries. And Vee's famous apple fritters.

The next hours blurred into conversation and cake and someone attempting a karaoke song they absolutely should not have. The Brewhouse had that same warm, loud energy it always did on book club nights—but tonight it was something bigger.

At some point my parents waved goodnight from the iPad, promising they'd come visit soon so they could meet everyone properly.

The celebration kept rolling after that—more cake,

louder laughter, and people drifting between tables and the patio.

Eventually I slipped outside onto the patio for air.

The late summer night wrapped around me. Fireflies blinked near the tree line. The muffled hum of voices drifted out through the open door behind me.

I was only out there for a minute before someone stepped up behind me.

"Overwhelmed?" Caleb asked.

"In the best way."

His arms slid around my waist, pulling me back against his chest. Through the window, I could see Maggie and Sasha at the counter and a sleepy toddler curled up in a chair by the door.

I'd almost left all of this.

"I keep thinking about how close I came to missing it," I said quietly.

He pressed a kiss to the top of my head. "But you didn't."

"No." I turned in his arms and looked up at him. "And I didn't want a life that didn't include you."

"Good," he said softly. "Because I don't want a life without you either."

I wrapped my arms around him and rested my head against his chest. For a minute we just stood there, his heartbeat steady beneath my ear.

The door opened behind us, letting a burst of laughter spill onto the patio.

Through the window behind him, I could see the banner still hanging slightly crooked above the counter.

But it wasn't just about the contract.

Maplemoor had felt like home from the moment I arrived.

What I hadn't known then was how much life I would build here.

The women who knocked on my door when I didn't show up. The town that made room for me before I believed I belonged. And the man standing here with me now.

I lifted my head and kissed him softly.

Caleb rested his forehead against mine.

Inside The Brewhouse, our people laughed.

Home wasn't somewhere I ended up.

It was something we were building.

Together.

<h1 style="text-align:center">about the author</h1>

As a tween, Tina Gallagher and her best friend would create happily ever afters for their favorite soap opera couples. Eventually, the soap operas lost their appeal, but the writing never did.

Before living her dream as a full-time author, she worked a spectrum of jobs ranging from baking and cake decorating to marketing and project management.

In between creating memorable characters, traveling, and taking pole dance lessons, Tina enjoys spending time with her two grown children and Golden Irish named Thea.

www.ingramcontent.com/pod-product-compliance
Lightning Source LLC
Chambersburg PA
CBHW020917060726
47591CB00004B/1287